STILL OF THE NIGHT

A BURKE AND BLADE MYSTERY THRILLER
BOOK 6

MICHAEL LISTER

STILL OF THE NIGHT

A BURKE AND BLADE MYSTERY THRILLER
BOOK 6

MICHAEL LISTER

PULPWOOD PRESS

ALSO BY MICHAEL LISTER

Books by Michael Lister

(John Jordan Novels)

Power in the Blood

Blood of the Lamb

Flesh and Blood

(Special Introduction by Margaret Coel)

The Body and the Blood

Double Exposure

Blood Sacrifice

Rivers to Blood

Burnt Offerings

Innocent Blood

(Special Introduction by Michael Connelly)

Separation Anxiety

Blood Money

Blood Moon

Thunder Beach

Blood Cries

A Certain Retribution

Blood Oath

Blood Work

Cold Blood

Blood Betrayal

Blood Shot

Blood Ties

Blood Stone

Blood Trail

Bloodshed

Blue Blood

And the Sea Became Blood

The Blood-Dimmed Tide

Blood and Sand

A John Jordan Christmas

Blood Lure

Blood Pathogen

Beneath a Blood-Red Sky

Out for Blood

What Child is This?

(Jimmy Riley Novels)

The Big Goodbye

The Big Beyond

The Big Hello

The Big Bout

The Big Blast

(Merrick McKnight / Reggie Summers Novels)

Thunder Beach

A Certain Retribution

Blood Oath

Blood Shot

(Remington James Novels)

Double Exposure

(includes intro by Michael Connelly)

Separation Anxiety

Blood Shot

(Sam Michaels / Daniel Davis Novels)

Burnt Offerings

Blood Oath

Cold Blood

Blood Shot

(Love Stories)

Carrie's Gift

(Short Story Collections)

North Florida Noir

Florida Heat Wave

Delta Blues

Another Quiet Night in Desperation

(The Meaning Series)

Meaning Every Moment

The Meaning of Life in Movies

MORE: Do More of What Matters Most and Discover the Life of Your Dreams

For Bob
From grateful, grateful parts!

CHAPTER
ONE

"TELL ME WHY WE DOIN' this again," Blade says.

Her words ricochet off the concrete and steel of the stairwell and echo around us.

"I have to see her."

We are inside of West Florida Medical Center sneaking up to Lexi's room.

Blade, an African-American woman in her mid-twenties, is built like a collegiate linebacker and usually dresses like a boss ass biker bitch, but today is in pale green scrubs that fit her powerful frame like green-tinted Glad Cling Wrap.

Apart from being raised in the system together and both being PIs we're about as different as two people can get, but we're family in a way that's unquantifiable and I can count on her more than any other soul on the planet.

"You get caught and you ain't gonna be seein' anyone for a long time," she says. "Your new probation officer can't take a joke for shit."

This little ill-advised stunt is a violation of my probation, but I haven't seen Lexi since she got shot and her family refuses to give me any updates on her condition.

"That's why you're here," I say.

"So now my job description includes keepin' your ass out of prison?"

"It came with your promotion and pay raise."

She laughs and it rises up into the open space above us and reverberates around like an aural lottery ball.

Lexi Miller, my former probation officer who I was having an affair with, was kidnapped by an unhinged Russian mobster named Dimitri and shot as we tried to rescue her. She has been in a coma ever since, and there are few things I can think of that I feel more guilty about.

She's in MI5—the Medical Intensive Care Unit located on the 5th floor.

When we reach the 5th floor, we pause a moment to catch our breath and calm ourselves, and then open and step through the large, heavy metal door.

The long, dully lit hallway is all smooth, hard sanitized surfaces. To our right are the locked double doors of ICU, about halfway down is the nurses' station, and on the opposite end is the physical therapy gym.

Most of the patient rooms doors are closed. A few empty carts, a recliner and a hospital bed in need of repair are not far from the entrance to the ICU waiting room where a few family members are seated in uncomfortable chairs, a couple of small, sad Christmas trees, and a gaunt African-American man is standing at the window talking quietly on his phone.

A few visitors, a couple of nurses, and a doctor are moving about, the nurses pushing their portable workstations.

As I scan the area, I'm hit with a cacophony of sounds and smells.

The beeping of IV pumps, the wheels of portable computer stations and housekeeping carts being rolled down the hall, disembodied voices—some somber and hushed, others irate, still others jovial and laced with laughter—daytime TV shows, Christmas carols, elevator doors, the tapping of keyboards, the dinging of bells, the buzzing of alarms, and the occasional PA pages of calls and codes.

As my ears take in all the discrepant and desultory sounds, my olfactory senses are assaulted by the metallic acrid odor of blood, which I not only smell but taste, the citrus bleachy smell of cleaning products, the aroma of breakfast, including the smokey smell of bacon, the foul stench of human excrement, the floral scents of soap, shampoo, and body lotion, the tang of body odor, urine, and the discordant, indefinable fragrance of illness and antiseptic.

We've come at shift change, hoping it will be too early for other family members to be visiting and the newly on-duty nurses will be too busy to realize we're not family.

Entry to MI5 is via a keypad, which we don't have the code for, but the doors are electronic and remain open a few moments after someone enters so we're hoping to slip in that way.

"We can't just stand here like this," Blade says. "We look sus as fuck."

"I know. Let's— "

A very tall housekeeping cart of fresh, sterilized linens is working its way down the hall.

I nod toward it.

"If that is headed into ICU," I say, "we can go in right after it and be hidden behind it. Let's go back into the stairwell and wait for it to get down here."

"Yeah, our asses a lot less conspicuous loitering in the stairwell."

"You just worry about changing those bedpans, Nurse Blade. I'll get us in ICU."

We loiter in the stairwell for a few minutes, and then I sneak a peek into the hallway again.

"The linen cart is almost here," I say. "You ready?"

"To get caught 'cause this ain't gonna work? Yeah, I'm ready."

I watch as the heavyset young white man wheels the large cart up to the ICU doors and taps the code onto the keypad.

His pale thick mitt of a hand eclipses the keypad so I can't see what the code is.

The electronic doors slowly open and he even more slowly ambles back over to his cart and begins to ease inside.

Blade who is beside me now says, "His fat ass is movin' too slow. Doors gonna close before we can get in."

"Let's go," I say.

I pull open the door and step out into the hallway, Blade right behind me.

By the time we near the ICU doors, they are beginning to close.

"Go fast," Blade says, "but don't look like you're runnin'."

"Oh, okay," I say. "Thanks for that."

We slip inside the ICU just as the doors are closing, the one on the left bumping into me and Blade careening off the one on the right.

We are mostly hidden by the large man and his tall linen cart.

As I lean around him and his cart to scope out ICU I see that the nurses' station, a long counter with computer centers on each side, directly in front of us, is empty, and that all seven rooms are full. The two nurses and a physical therapist are working with patients.

I can't tell from here which room Lexi is in.

We're going to have to go to each one to find her, which is going to make us more conspicuous and give more opportunities for us to get caught.

The large man and his large linen cart veer to the left and we follow.

The first room holds an old white man with no teeth and gray stubble on his sunken cheeks.

"I'm gonna walk around to the other rooms on this side and see if I can find her," I whisper to Blade. "You stay here and keep an eye out."

"Ten-four."

I attempt to walk to the next room like I know what I'm doing and am supposed to be there.

An elderly woman snoring loudly is in it.

As I'm about to move to the next room, one of the nurses announces she's going to get a patient's meds from the pneumatic tube at the nurses' station on the regular part of the floor.

I wait until she leaves and then head to the next room and find Lexi.

My breath catches in my chest.

I am unprepared for what seeing her on a ventilator and IV pump does to me.

She looks so pale and frail, so vulnerable.

It's as if she's already gone.

I move up beside her and take her hand.

Kissing it I tell her how sorry I am I let this happen.

"If we had never met or never got involved . . . this wouldn't've happened to you."

Her eyes move beneath their lids and I wonder if it's some sort of response.

"Fight," I say. "Please. Please don't stop until you claw your way out of this. Do everything you can. Fight with all you have. I know that's enough. I know it is. Wake up. Come back. Please."

"Sir, visiting hours haven't started yet."

I turn toward the nurse standing in the entryway wiping tears from my eyes.

I nod.

Seeing my tears softens her and she says, "Just a few more moments, okay?"

"Thank you."

I turn back toward Lexi and a moment later the nurse is beside me.

"Tell her you want her to live," she whispers. "She needs to hear y'all say it. Tell her just how much y'all want her to still be here. Tell her to come back to ya'll. Tell her when they take her off the ventilator she has to fight harder than she ever has in her entire life."

I feel my heart plummet.

I had no idea they were taking her off the ventilator, but I try not to show it.

I nod. "Thank you."

She pats me on the arm and eases out of the room.

I lean down and place my mouth at Lexi's ear, my lips grazing her skin as I speak. "Please don't die. Please. You've got . . . Your life is just getting started. This isn't right. Do it for me too. Don't make me carry this around the rest of my life, that I got you killed. Please."

Blade coughs loudly and I turn to see Lexi's Mom and sister entering the ward.

If they see me they'll report me and I'll go back to prison for violation of probation.

I kiss Lexi's hand and slip out of the room.

I start to turn left and go around the opposite way I came in but the entire ward is so open they'd see me if they glanced in that direction.

To my right I see that the tall linen cart is parked in front of the room next to Lexi's.

If I time it right maybe I can be on one side of the cart while they pass by on the other.

It's my only chance.

Blade is still over by the entrance having her coughing fit. Her head is down and her face can't be seen.

The large linen cart man is in the room next to me.

I duck behind the linen cart and kneel down as if I'm tying my shoe, hoping no one sees me, let alone realizes my shoes don't have laces.

Suddenly, the big guy is directly behind me, dirty linens draped across his arms.

I turn my head and look up at him. "Something in my shoe, sorry," I say.

"No problem," he says in a shockingly high, soft voice.

I slip off my shoe trying to delay a few moments longer before I get up.

I hear Lexi's mom and sister pass by on the other side of the cart and quickly slip my shoe back on, hop up, and begin to walk toward the exit.

"Hey," Lexi's mom says.

I keep walking and don't turn around.

"Yes, ma'am," the big guy says in an even higher pitched voice.

"Can you change her sheets later after we're gone?"

"Sure, yes ma'am."

As Blade and I exit ICU, the nurse returning with the meds gives Blade a strange look, but seeing that I've been crying nods toward me with a sympathetic expression and keeps moving.

As do we, through the door to our left, down the stairwell, and out of the building.

CHAPTER
TWO

"MAYBE SHE'LL COME out of it," Blade is saying.

We are back in her vehicle, a new black SUV with the blackout package—black rims, black grille, all emblems and badges removed. We are headed east toward Panama City. She's driving. I'm deep inside myself in the passenger seat.

"She stronger than she look," she adds. "Lot stronger than your average skinny ass blond white girl."

I don't respond.

"Don't revise history," she says. "You know you ain't been that into her lately. Been far more into the mom."

The mom is how she refers to Heather Harrison because she's so much older than me. I've been involved with Lexi since not long after I got out, but started seeing Heather when we worked her daughter's case. Neither entanglement was ideal. Lexi was my probation officer and not only was it against every rule for us to be involved but it risked her job and my freedom. Heather is broken from the loss of her daughter and old enough to be my mother. But I care very deeply for them both.

I shake my head.

"What?" she says. "It's true and you know it."

She's right. Lexi and I had cooled off some, and shortly

before she was shot she told me she couldn't be involved with me any longer because it hurt too much to watch me self-destruct, but she had said something similar before and we hadn't stopped seeing each other.

"I just feel so . . . guilty. What happened to Lexi is my fault."

"Bet you're tellin' yourself there's no way you can see the mom now, aren't you?"

I nod. "I could never—"

"I knew it. I may not know my self for shit, but I know you. You predictable as hell. You plan on punishin' yourself for the rest of your life? Just curious about the coming attractions I got to look forward to."

I don't say anything.

"I know I'm wasting my fuckin' breath, but what happened to Lexi is on Dimitri and only on Dimitri. And I'm the one who humiliated his bitch ass. And I only had to do that to save your ass 'cause fuckin' Logan Owens' paranoid ass had you vettin' his little stripper hooker. So it's actually on Owens. And . . . not for nothin' but every bad thing that has happened to you in past few years is on that sick albino prick. And yet we workin' for his creepy little ass again."

Logan Owens is the reason I went to prison.

I have anger issues. I sometimes explode. And my series of assaults and my many simple batteries and my general history of violence meant that when I was charged with aggravated battery for beating Logan Owens nearly to death, I was charged with a felony and sent to prison. Because my sentencing score sheet was so high, the judge sentenced me to a year and a day of state prison time, followed by two years of probation. If I ever violate my probation, I'll return to prison to serve my full sentence as well as any additional time I might pick up from the act that violated me back in the first place.

As far as the legal system is concerned Logan is my victim—though he's never been anything but a victimizer—and one of the conditions of my probation is to have no contact with him.

As fucked up as it is, I work for Owens from time to time because he has video evidence that would both send me back and add time to my sentence and he's blackmailing me with it.

One of the assignments he had me do was investigate a stripper named Destiny he was involved with before he married her.

Shortly before they were to be married she vanished off the face of the earth and now he's having me search for her, which I would've done anyway because I feel responsible for her and I suspect him of being behind her disappearance.

"Shit's ironic as hell too," she says. "We findin' her for him when we both know he's the one who's behind her disappearance."

"Probably is," I say, "but why have us try to find her?"

"To see if we can find her," she says. "He's testin' how good he hid her body and covered his tracks before the cops get involved. He knows if we can't find her nobody can."

"Which is why we've got to find her."

CHAPTER
THREE

WHEN WE PULL into the parking lot of the law firm where our office is, Logan Owens is waiting for us.

After we park and get out of our vehicle, Clyde Broussard, Owens' bodyguard and our sometime secret conspirator, gets out of the dark ash-gray metallic Chevy Tahoe with illegally tinted windows so black nothing can be seen inside.

The December day is cool and bright with very little humidity, traffic is light on 15th Street, and the businesses across the street have festive Christmas decorations adorning their store fronts.

"Mr. Owens would like a word," he says.

When Clyde is around Owens, he is formal and distant and acts as if we have no relationship outside of this one.

Blade says, "I got a word for him."

I nod and step toward the huge SUV.

Blade follows.

"Not you," Clyde says.

"Why not *me*?" she says.

"Mr. Owens is concerned you will cut him if given even half a chance."

"He's wrong," she says.

"Is he?"

"Wasn't finished. He's wrong about a lot of shit . . . but he ain't wrong about that."

Clyde nods to himself.

"I'll catch up with you inside," I say.

She doesn't move, just stands there watching as Clyde opens the door for me and I, once again, violate my probation and climb into the back of the SUV.

The backseat of the huge vehicle is about the size of a small apartment.

I sink into the plush leather seat as Clyde climbs back into the driver's seat, the entire vehicle leaning toward the enormity of him.

Clyde raises the dark tinted glass partition and I glance over at Owens.

He's a young, thin, pale white man with freakishly light blue eyes and wild bleached-blond hair.

He's staring straight ahead and refuses to make eye contact with me.

When Owens had me investigate Destiny the first time, I had gone to see her at Cloud Nine Gentlemen's Club. After tipping her on the stage, she came over to see me at my table and we had eventually made our way to a VIP room in the back where she gave me the girlfriend experience and her number.

Destiny is her stripper name. Heather is the name on her voicemail. But we now know her actual name is Charlotte Nelson.

She doesn't look like a Charlotte. She's a tall, thin, leggy platinum blonde with plenty of long hair extensions, massive fake mammaries, a smooth airbrush spray tan, and makeup that appears professionally applied. At least she was the last time I saw her. I have no idea what she looks like now. I'm just hoping she's not a decaying corpse in a shallow grave somewhere.

"Have you found her yet?" he asks.

"We just started looking."

"I understand the first forty-eight hours are the most crucial."

"That clock starts the moment someone goes missing, not when we start our investigation. She was missing far more than forty-eight when you came to us."

"I thought maybe she just got cold feet or something. Figured Clyde could find her. Had I known she was . . . Had I had a better grasp of the circumstances . . . I would have taken a different approach."

"Hindsight, am I right?"

He gives me a little growl to express his displeasure at my remark.

I can see why Clyde is so formal when around Owens. He gets it from Owens. Every word is measured. His voice is devoid of emotion and gives no indication we even have a history—let alone such a fraught one. He's playing a part and refuses to break character.

It's disconcerting to be this close and conversing with the predator I was sent to prison for hospitalizing. It's surreal to be working for him, even if it's to keep from going back to prison.

"You have nothing for me?" he says. "No leads? No news? Nothing to report?"

"Not yet. It's early days. We'll have something soon."

"In case I haven't been clear," he says. "This is to be your first and only priority. I want you to find her . . . not eventually, but as soon as humanly possible. Understand? This matters more to me than anything. Ever. I expect results. I keep hearing how good you two are . . . Makes me think maybe you're not taking my case seriously."

"That's not the case," I say. "Even if you hadn't brought this to us, if I heard she was missing I'd look for her. But these cases take time. Especially a case like this when there's nothing to go on."

"If you don't get results soon, I'm going to turn over the evidence I have on you to the authorities and hire another firm to find her. You can read about where she was found from inside prison."

CHAPTER
FOUR

"OH, y'all are going to love this case," Pete is saying. "It's like it was designed especially for you."

He unlocks the door and leads us into Charlotte Nelson's apartment.

Pistol Pete Anderson is an investigator with the Bay County Sheriff's Office. He's also one of our foster brothers. He's a lean, clean-cut late-twenties man with pale skin and short reddish-blond hair.

"She's in the void," he adds. "Vanished off the face of the earth without a trace. No witnesses. No evidence. No signs of her since."

Charlotte's apartment complex, the Sunset Palms, is located on Back Beach and bills itself as a luxury apartment community with convenience and comfort all in one. Claiming it's not just a home but a lifestyle, its expansive amenities include a fitness center, hardwood flooring, private patios, in-home washer and dryer, walk-in closets, high ceilings, a business center, a club-house, a Coffee Bar, and olympic size swimming pool with a poolside veranda, and an outdoor fireplace and grill area.

We step inside Charlotte's bright, spotless apartment and are greeted with the rich, sweet, fruity, floral, sensual smell of Jasmine.

We are standing on carbonized antiqued bamboo hand-scraped laminate flooring in a two-story foyer. To our left is a carpeted staircase with a wrought iron banister. To our right is the smallish kitchen. Directly in front of us is the downstairs bathroom.

"Who filed the missing person report?" I ask.

He opens the folder he's holding. "Keisha Barjon."

Blade says, "Need to talk to her. Who is she?"

"Friend," he says. "Co-worker."

"At Cloud Nine?" Blade says.

"No, I don't think so."

"She worked somewhere else too?" I ask.

"Evidently," he says, and looks back at the report in the open folder. "KLS, Incorporated."

"What's that?" Blade asks.

He shrugs. "No idea."

"What kind of stripper has a day job?" Blade says.

"None I've ever met," Pete says.

"Met a lot of strippers, have you?" she says.

"Well, there's Ashlynn," he says.

Ashlynn is our foster sister and Alana's mom, and, yes, he knows her, but knows nothing about her work and has never been in a strip club.

"This one has a day job at a mysterious place *and* a sugar daddy," Blade says. "Might be more to her than I thought."

I nod. "Her place isn't what I expected."

"No, it's not," she says. "It's nice and clean and orderly."

The apartment has a townhouse feel, narrow and high. The first floor holds the kitchen, dining, and living room, with a bedroom and bathroom on the second and third floors.

"We each take a floor we get done faster," Blade says.

I nod. "I'll take the top floor."

Blade says, "Pete you take this one and I'll take the second."

Clean white walls dominate every floor. As if blank canvasses, they are empty—no pictures or paintings, no nails or patches in the sheetrock. The rare places where there are paintings— two each over the couch and beds—they are of the large, mass produced, bland big box store type.

Unlike many of her neighbors, Charlotte has no Christmas decorations up.

Her bedroom is huge and sparsely decorated. A navy-blue nautical themed comforter matches a little too perfectly the paintings hanging over the bed and the rugs and shower curtain in the master bathroom, as if they were purchased as part of a set.

Her bed is made. Her bathroom is immaculate. Her large walk-in closet is orderly.

Nothing is out of place. Nothing.

Her suitcase is under the bed and it appears that all of her makeup and hair and skin products are in the bathroom.

The book beneath the lamp on her bedside table is "A Girl's Guide to Getting it Right."

The drawer in the nightstand holds, among other random things, a handgun and a vibrator.

As I'm standing in her bedroom and thinking about her, I realize something about Charlotte reminds me of someone, but the more I think about it the more I can't come up with who it could be.

After a thorough look around during which I find nothing of interest, I meet the others downstairs in the foyer.

"Doesn't really look like anyone lives here, does it?" Pete says.

"Even the personal things seem impersonal," I say.

Blade says, "Could just be 'cause she's got a cold, cold heart."

"It's odd," I say. "It almost seems staged, like it's a display model, but you can tell she lives here."

"Maybe she's just a clean freak," Pete says. "And with two

jobs and a boyfriend wasn't here a lot. Maybe mostly livin' at his place."

"It looks like all her makeup and hygiene products are still here," I say. "And her clothes and suitcase. And her gun and her vibrator. Doesn't appear that she packed."

"She didn't go off on her own," Blade says. "Might leave everything else but she wouldn't've left her vibrator."

"What's the story with her cell phone and banking?" I ask Pete.

"Hasn't touched any of her money—and she's got some," he says. "Twenty-thousand in savings. Five in checking. Haven't been able to track her phone. And haven't found anything belonging to her—not her purse, phone, car, anything."

"Car's hard to hide," Blade says. "Maybe she did a runner and is in her car far away from here. Probably gettin' the hell away from Owens."

"We've got a BOLO out on her," Pete says. "If she's out there in her vehicle, we'll find her."

I shake my head. "Almost impossible to intentionally disappear."

"Yeah, true, but . . . she worked in a cash business. No tellin' how much she socked away."

"Don't know if it has any bearing on her disappearance," Pete says, "but she took a trip the week before it happened."

"Where'd she go?" Blade asks.

"St. Simon's Island."

"Do we know what for?" I ask.

He shrugs. "Not sure yet. Still trying to find out."

"Are we sure she came back?" I ask.

"We have a few different witnesses sayin' she did."

"But . . ." Blade says. "Doesn't mean she did."

"True," he says. "I'm trying to get some confirmation."

Blade shakes her head and smirks. "This case already more interestin' than I ever thought it could be."

CHAPTER
FIVE

KLS, Incorporated is located in a relatively new light industrial park not far from downtown Panama City.

Billing itself as a fully planned and restricted industrial park located near beautiful downtown Panama City, the Bay County Commerce Park is a dual-use development that provides prime locations for both light-industrial and office/distribution tenants.

Much of the newish park is still unoccupied, its enormous buildings dormant, empty.

KLS, Incorporated occupies an office/distribution hub and is the only facility in the park surrounded by a high chain-link fence on top of which is looping strands of razor wire.

I park in a mostly empty lot about twenty yards from KLS and get out.

It's a dark night. The temperature has dropped, and the air is cool and thin.

As if not wanting to be noticed, the building KLS is housed in is dim. The only illumination is a faint glow from a loading dock in the back.

Red security camera lights blink from their many positions along the perimeter fence and the building.

The building is set back about twenty feet from the fence and the entrance consists of both a steel rolling gate on a track for vehicles and an electronic pedestrian gate with a black keypad callbox on a metal stand bolted to the concrete a few feet in front of it.

As I approach the callbox, a bright security light blinks on, illuminating me and the area around me.

A raspy male voice from the callbox speaker says, "This is private property. You are trespassing."

"I'm looking for Charlotte Nelson."

"This is not a place you look for people in," he says. "And there's no one here by that name."

"How about Keisha Barjon?"

"See previous answer."

"What is your name?"

He doesn't respond.

"I'm a private detective working a missing person case," I say. "My name is Lucas Burke. Could I come in and talk to you about—"

"No."

"It won't take but—"

"Leave now or you'll be escorted away."

I find it interesting that he didn't say he'd get the police involved.

"Maybe I could speak to the person who comes to escort me away," I say. "I just have a few questions."

"Leave now or else."

"Or else what?" I ask.

No response.

"What is KLS?" I ask. "What do y'all do? Why all the security?"

"Final warning," he says. "Leave on your own or be removed."

The bright light blinks off and I'm momentarily blinded.

I continue to ask questions for several more minutes but don't receive a response for any of them.

Eventually, I sense someone in the darkness behind me and spin around.

No one is directly behind me and it's too dark to make out anyone in the area, but I know someone is there.

"I'm just a boy standing in front of a dark figure looking for a girl," I say.

I can hear breathing. There's more than one person in the darkness.

Then I hear the unmistakable sound of the slide of a semi-automatic handgun being pulled back and released to chamber a round.

"Like I said, I'm just a boy standing in front of armed dark figures asking them to let me leave."

A very low voice whispers, "Go now and don't come back."

CHAPTER
SIX

I'M SITTING at the end of the bar by myself not far from the smaller, second stage in Cloud Nine.

I came here after leaving KLS. It's early in club terms—a little after eleven—and the crowd is still relatively small.

The two stages of Cloud Nine are rectangular with a pole on each end and are located out in the middle of the floor so patrons can stand on all sides.

As usual, it's loud and cold and smells of body lotion, booze, and cigarette smoke.

Declan is working the door and Winston is in the back at the entrance to the VIP section. Both men, twenty-something African-Americans—are enormous with plenty of both fat and muscle, their masses barely being held back by their 5XL white shirts and black vests.

The relentless beat of the banging house music is bland and boring, and I yawn as I take another sip of my drink.

Crystal is on the side stage not far from me with a few customers standing around tipping her.

Grabbing my stack of ones, I climb off the barstool and approach the stage.

At the three-minute mark of "I Luv Dem Strippers," the unseen DJ fades it down and brings up "Rocket."

I step over to the far side of the stage and stand there by myself, waiting my turn. When she finishes being tipped by the other men here to admire her, she makes her way over to me.

She's all legs, augmented breasts, and black hair extensions. Her skin is milky white, which contrasts nicely with her dark hair, and both her pale skin and her black hair cause her crystal-blue eyes to appear to be lit with pin spotlights that follow her wherever she goes.

I make eye contact with her and give her a smile.

As she starts her routine, I keep my eyes locked onto hers.

"That's an intense gaze you got, honey," she says.

"Your eyes are . . . extraordinary."

"You should see the rest of me."

I let my eyes take in her long, tall body for a moment and then come right back to her eyes.

Soon she is down to only a black G-string and eight-inch clear acrylic platform heels.

I'm holding a large stack of ones and have yet to tip her.

"What's a girl got to do to get some of those?" she asks, nodding toward the wad of cash.

"They're all yours already," I say.

I place them down in a neat stack on the stage beside her.

"That's different," she says.

Most guys toss or sling their money onto the girls. Some actually throw it at them.

"Thank you, honey," she says. "I'll come see you when I get done."

I walk back over to the bar and take my seat.

As I sip on my drink and she rolls around on the stage, lifting and spreading her legs, shaking her ass, and placing her plastic breasts in customers' faces, I notice her throwing occasional glances my way.

When she completes her set, she cleans the poles, gathers her tips, and gets dressed. And then heads over to me.

"Thank you, honey," she says, hugging me. "Can I join you?"

I nod and gesture toward the seat beside me. "What would you like to drink?"

"Long Island Iced Tea, please," she says.

I give the order to the hovering bartender.

"Thank you, handsome," she says. "How are you tonight?"

"Better now," I say, and I'm a little surprised by just how flat and insincere I sound.

The bartender returns with Crystal's drink and I pay her and tell her to keep the change.

"Cheers," she says.

"Salut."

"How's your day goin'?" she asks.

"I've had better," I say. "Yours?"

She shrugs. "Okay."

We spend the next ten minutes or so in banal small talk and then she pops the question.

"Would you like to continue this in the privacy of VIP?" she asks.

"I would."

I give her money for the room and she goes and pays for it, and in less than a minute we are making our way to the back.

VIP is the section in the back reserved for private dances. It's a dim hallway with small rooms off to one side, each with beaded curtains instead of doors so security can keep an eye on the activities going on inside of them.

Winston is surprised to see me. Beneath raised eyebrows he gives me a smile. "Burke," he says.

"Winston."

"Been a while," he says. "Surprised to see you here."

"Surprised to be here."

Inside the small, mirrored booth, she sits me down on the built-in cushioned seat and starts undressing.

When she has stripped down to only her T-back G-string, she moves me to the center of the seat and straddles me.

"Just stay like that," I say.

"Okay."

"I'll give you two-hundred dollars just to sit like that and talk to me for a few minutes."

"Sure, okay, baby, whatever you want, but I can't have sex with you."

"I'm a PI. I've been hired to find Destiny."

"Really?" she says, the pitch of her voice rising. "I could tell you were different."

"Any idea where Destiny is?" I ask.

She shakes her head. "She went on a trip last week, but—"

"Did you see her when she came back?"

"Yeah."

"How'd she seem?"

"She's been different lately. Not sure why. Just like . . . I don't know . . . more quiet, to herself."

"Did she say anything about the trip?"

"Not really. Said it was nice. But that's about it."

"Do you know why she went or what she did?"

She shakes her head. "I probably know more about her than anyone here and I know next to nothing about her. She's very . . . private."

Someone passes by in the hallway and she moves around a bit, pretending to be dancing for me.

"She . . . It's like she's a lot of different people—or can be. I guess workin' here we all are a little, but she . . . She was next level. I never knew who the real her was. Guess I didn't meet her."

"She say much about her boyfriend?" I ask.

"No. It was so strange. He was in here one time with her and said something about them getting married and that was the first time any of us had heard about it. She's fuckin' engaged and never even mentioned it. We just thought she was givin' him the boyfriend experience like everyone else and then out of nowhere she's going to marry him. It was bizarre."

"Did she say why she was marrying him?"

She shakes her head. "But we all knew. Only one reason you marry someone like him. The money."

I start to say something but she takes a big inhale and I wait.

"You know how some people are good actors?" she asks.

"Yeah?"

"You know how you know they're good actors?" she says. "Because you see how they are when they're not acting. Right? But with Destiny . . . it's like she was always acting. Always playing a role. Always in character. I know her better than anyone here and I don't know her at all."

"Did she ever—"

A large Russian man with a big black beard pushes through the bead curtain, grabs Crystal by the arm, and lifts her up.

"Get your things and get back to work," he says.

Unlike Dimitri and Bogdan he has very little Russian accent.

She does as she's told, quickly gathering her things .

When I try to stand he pushes me back down onto the seat.

Withdrawing a handgun from a shoulder holster beneath his coat he points it at me.

I lift my hands and sit back in the seat.

"You got some big brass balls comin' back in here," he says. "Kill Dimitri and just waltz back in here like it's nothing."

"I didn't have the pleasure of killing Dimitri," I say, "but the person who did, did so in self-defense."

"I'm going to enjoy killin' the piss out of you," he says. He presses the barrel of the .9mm or .45 into the center of my forehead. "I can put a bullet in your brain right now and no one in here will hear it."

He's right. The pounding house music will muffle most of the bang of the discharge, especially if it's a .9.

"I thought we did y'all a favor by takin' him out," I say. "Didn't you all move up the food chain?"

. . .

Winston appears in the doorway behind him. "Everything okay in here?"

"Just havin' a little conversation with this big-balled bastard."

"I'll escort him out and make sure he never comes back," Winston says.

"I got this," the big Russian says.

"He's connected to the cops," Winston says. "There's one out there looking for him right now. You don't want that kind of heat. Let me just throw him out. And I guarantee he won't be back."

CHAPTER
SEVEN

"YOUR ASS GOT guns pulled on you twice in one night?"
Blade says.

"It's a gift," I say. "And a personal best. I've had two guns
pulled on me in one night before but not at different times in
different situations."

We are standing in our kitchen. I've just come from Cloud
Nine and she has just come in from a date.

She says, "If not for Winston I'd be looking for a new partner
tomorrow."

A few weeks ago Ashlynn, Alana, Blade, and I had moved in
together. We're renting a place on 11th Court in St. Andrews. The
converted house, which is walking distance from Beck, is split
into three sections. Blade is in the part that used to be an Airbnb.
I'm in the middle section that, in addition to my bedroom and
bathroom, includes the kitchen and living room. Ashlynn and
Alana are in the part that was once a mother-in-law suite.

"How bad did seein' Lexi and hearin' they're pullin' the plug
fuck you up?" she asks.

I shrug.

"That why you went into Cloud Nine like that? Unarmed. No
backup. You ain't been that reckless since Alana was born."

"Didn't really think about it," I say.

"Well, think about it."

I do.

She's right and her point is well taken.

Eventually, I nod. "I'm more fucked up than I realized."

"Well, get your shit together before it gets you killed. Do it for Alana if not for yourself."

I nod.

A moment of heavy silence passes between us.

I take a deep breath and let it out slowly.

"So," she says, her voice changing back to its usual upbeat, edgy timbre, "the fuck is inside KLS that makes it so valuable? They gonna shoot your ass just for bein' in the parkin' lot."

"Both places Charlotte worked are dangerous and had her around armed bad guys," I say. "Maybe—"

"Luc, my tummy is hurtin'."

I turn to see Alana standing at the entrance of the kitchen squinting up at me in her Princess Jasmine nightgown.

I quickly step over to her and pick her up. Hugging her to me I move over toward the medicine cabinet.

"Let's get you some medicine and some water," I say. "What's it feel like?"

"Night Alana," Blade says as she heads toward her side of the house. "Night Dr. Burke."

"Night, Blade," Alana says in a soft, sweet, sleepy voice that melts me.

Setting Alana down on the counter, I open the cabinet, withdraw a single antacid tablet and give it to her.

She begins sucking on it like hard candy.

"Chew it up and swallow it," I say. "We want to get it into your tummy as quickly as we can."

She does.

Picking her back up I carry her to the fridge and grab a cold water bottle.

"Drink this," I say. "It'll help."

"I don't like water."

"I know, but it will help your tummy. I promise. Drink as much as you can. You don't have to drink it all."

"Can we watch the big scream?"

The big scream is how she refers to the large TV in the living room after hearing me call it the big screen.

"For a few minutes, then we need to get back to bed."

We sit together on the couch, her snuggled up next to me beneath her Toy Story blanket and watch the homemade Youtube videos featuring little girls about her age she loves so much.

Soon she is back asleep and I am happy I didn't get shot tonight and miss this.

CHAPTER
EIGHT

THE NEXT MORNING I attend an anger management group, and though it is court ordered I would go even if it weren't. I have no problem saying my name and confessing that I'm a rage-ohalic. I know I have a problem. And not just with anger issues. I'm broken in a way that only an orphan raised in the system can be. But I've become convinced that my fucked-up-ness is not my fate. I can get better and I intend to. Hell, I already am. Slowly. And not in a particularly pretty way. But I see progress nonetheless.

Later this morning, Blade and I are driving over to St. Simon's Island to see if we can find out why Charlotte went there the week before she vanished and to see if it has anything to do with her disappearance.

Even after the meeting I'm keyed up and agitated.

Not knowing whether Lexi is dead or not and not being able to find out makes me want to smash some shit up. I'm hurting and I want to hurt something or someone, to spread this pain and grief and anger, to infect someone else with this disease.

I call Pete from my car after the meeting.

"Morning," he says.

"Can you find out if they pulled the plug on Lexi for me?" I ask.

"I can try," he says. "Problem is most everyone knows I'm asking for you and it can get me in trouble."

"I don't want to cause you any issues," I say, "but if there's a way you can find out without any blowback on you I'd really appreciate it."

"Of course," he says. "I'll see what I can do. And , man, I'm sorry as hell it happened and you're goin' through this."

"Thanks, brother. I appreciate it."

After disconnecting the call, I sit there for a moment and take a few deep breaths.

Why does everything have to be so fucked? Why was I born to such shitty parents? Why did I have to go through so much? Why do pricks like Logan Owens get away with so much? He's like a Jeffery Epstein on a local level. Why was I sent to prison for trying to stop him? Why did I have to get involved with Lexi and get her killed?

Why? Why? Why?

No answers come. They never do.

My phone rings and I quickly lift it up hoping it's Pete with news of Lexi.

It's Heather Harrison.

I don't want to take her call, but I've avoided her long enough.

"Hey," I say.

"What're you doin?" she says.

"Feeling sorry for myself and questioning the nature of the fuckin' universe."

"*Fu-un,*" she says. "I'd love to hear all about it. Can you meet me for breakfast?"

"Sorry, can't today," I say.

"There a reason you're avoiding me ?"

I start to say no but then decide to tell her the truth. We've always been mostly honest with each other.

"I certainly understand," she says. "You know I do. I went for years not being able to do anything pleasurable."

"I should've told you sooner. Should've known you'd understand."

"I'm just glad you told me now. Look, I'm here. Let me know if and when I can do anything. And know this . . . we don't have to do anything pleasurable or guilt-producing. We can just talk and let me check on you."

"Thanks."

As soon as I'm off the phone with Heather, I text Pete.

Find out anything?

Not yet. May take me a little while. I'll let you know something as soon as I know.

Okay. Thanks. And sorry.

A few moments later, Blade calls and says, "Let's ride."

CHAPTER
NINE

WE TAKE I-10 East through Tallahassee and Jacksonville and then I-95 up to Brunswick.

With quick stops at Blaze Pizza in Tallahassee and the Busy Bee near Live Oak, it takes us about five hours.

Crossing over the Brunswick River on the stunning Sidney Lanier Bridge we take in the vast expanse of marsh land that dominates the area. The enormous and striking bridge, which provides access to the Golden Isles from I-95, and is named for the poet who devoted his work to the region, is the tallest and longest cable-stayed bridge in the state at 7,780-feet long and 486-feet tall.

In a few more minutes we are crossing the four-mile causeway to the island.

St. Simons island, which is roughly the size of Manhattan, is a seventeen square mile barrier island off the coast of Georgia.

During the chiefdom era, the Guale Indians established a chiefdom on St. Catherines Island and used St. Simons for hunting and fishing, but by 1500 had established a permanent village here also.

Beginning around 1568 the Spanish created missions along the Georgia coast which led to the assimilations of the indige-

nous people here. By the 1600s St. Simons was home to two
Spanish missions—San Buenaventura de Guadalquini, on the
southern tip and Santo Domingo de Asao on the northern one.
But in1684 pirate raids left the missions and villages largely
ghost towns.

By 1733 General James Edward Oglethorpe founded the
English settlement of Savannah. In 1736 he established Fort Frederica, named after the heir to the British throne, Frederick Louis,
Prince of Wales, on the west side of St. Simons in an attempt to
safeguard Savannah and the Carolinas from the Spanish threat.

By the time of the American Revolution, Fort Frederica was
obsolete, and St. Simons was left largely uninhabited.

Following the Revolutionary War, the island was transformed
into fourteen cotton plantations after acres of live oak trees were
cleared for farmland and used for building American warships,
including the famous USS Constitution often referred to as Old
Ironsides for the way cannon balls bounced off the huge St.
Simons' timbers it was constructed from. During this time, St.
Simons was known for its production of long-staple cotton,
which soon came to be known as Sea Island cotton, and in the
years leading up to the Civil War its plantations flourished.

In 1924 the Brunswick–St. Simons Highway, now known as
the Torras Causeway, begin to transform St. Simons into the
resort community it is today.

According to a statement given by Keisha to the Bay County
Sheriff's Office, when Charlotte came to St. Simons in the week
before her disappearance she stayed at Epworth by the Sea, a
Methodist retreat and conference center.

We drive straight there.

The entrance to riverside resort is beneath a canopy of enormous, ancient oak trees, their huge branches and limbs draped
with thick curtains of Spanish Moss.

And it's not just that oaks are so colossal but that they are so
plentiful as well.

Seeing the expansive, stately oaks causes my breath to catch in my chest. Their mammoth magnificence is soul-stirring. But the sight of them also fills me with deep sadness, a kind of homesickness for a home that no longer exists. Back in 2018, the Cat 5 super storm, Hurricane Michael, decimated our region of North Florida, obliterating many of our trees and leaving the ones that remain bowed and bent.

"The hell she doin' here?" Blade says.

"That's what we're here to find out," I say.

"This some sort of religious retreat center, right?"

"It is," I say, "but they host all sorts of non-religious events, corporate conferences, artistic retreats, weddings, parties, and various workshops. We need to find out which ones were going on when she was here and try to figure out which one she attended."

"This chick far more mysterious than I'd've ever guessed."

I nod my agreement.

"Hard to see this havin' anything to do with her disappearance," she says.

"I don't know . . . The timing is . . . suspicious."

"But if she made it back home safe and then disappeared . . ."

"Someone could've followed her from here," I say.

She shrugs. "Guess so. Anything's possible."

CHAPTER
TEN

THE ONLY PICTURE we have of Charlotte is one Owens gave us.

She has no online or social media presence we could find—not under her name or any of her aliases.

We find a youngish African-American man wearing a soiled apron and a hairnet by himself behind one of the kitchens.

Blade hands him the picture.

He takes it and studies it.

"Was she here last week?" she asks.

He nods. "Good looking woman," he says. "Stood out. Mostly we get old people and kids here."

"You talk to her?" I ask.

"Just to speak in passing," he says. "She thanked me for the food being good a time or two. That's about it."

I nod.

"Who y'all?" he asks. "Ain't cops."

"Private," I say. "Tryin' to find this woman."

"Well, she ain't still here," he says.

"You sure?" Blade asks.

He nods. "'Less she stopped eatin' and comin' out of her room."

"Do you know which room she had?" I ask.

He shakes his head.

"Could you find out for us?" Blade asks.

He hesitates.

"We'd really appreciate it," I say.

Blade adds, "And we'd be good friends to have if you ever get in a jam."

"I'll see what I can do."

"Was she here for an event?" I asks. "Part of a group?"

He nods. "Dining halls are assigned by group."

"Know which one she was part of?" Blades asks.

He shakes his head.

"Know which ones were here last week?"

He shakes his head again. "Can't keep up."

"Can you find out for us?"

"Can try."

"Have you done any time?" she asks.

He nods. "Is it that obvious?"

"Young black man cooking in a place like this," she says.

"Makes life more challenging, doesn't it?" I say.

He nods.

"You help us out with this and if you get in another jam you call us first," she says.

"Bet," he says, nodding. "Got a card or something?"

I hand him one. "I'm Burke. This is Blade."

"Theo," he says, tucking the card into his pocket. "Meet me back out here after nine tonight."

CHAPTER
ELEVEN

THE CAMPUS of Epworth by the Sea reminds me of an upscale summer camp. It's not quite nice enough to be classified as a resort, but it's better and bigger than most retreat centers I've seen.

The various buildings are mismatched and looked to have been built at different times without a unifying architectural vision. Contemporary hotels of differing styles are mixed in with summer camp style dorms, meeting halls, conference rooms, cafeteria style dining halls, and older chapels and buildings.

We walk down by the river as the sun begins its descent into evening.

The expansive waterway and surrounding marsh land has that hushed airy quality that large bodies of water get in calm late afternoons and evenings. I've experienced the same phenomena at the Gulf of Mexico and various lakes and rivers in North Florida.

To our left in the distance vehicles move in both directions over a rising stretch of the causeway, seen but not heard. To our right a man and a woman stand at the end of a cement pier fishing, beyond them a handful of boats are scattered about, appearing like a child's toys from this distance.

We are surrounded by serenity, a peaceful, meditative tableau, an outward atmosphere in stark contrast to my inward landscape.

I try to drink in the picturesque serenity, but we move on before it has much affect on me.

Turning to look back at the sprawling campus we see a large event tent set up on the green. Its logo reads Hope House: Supporting Families with Cancer.

A middle-aged white woman with frizzy dark hair is placing bottles of water and snacks onto folding tables with red plastic tablecloths on them.

We approach her.

"Important work y'all are doing," I say.

She nods gravely.

"Can't imagine," I say.

Her name is Marcy Ditmore. Says so right there on her name tag.

"There's literature on that table over there," she says. "Help yourself. What group are y'all here with?"

"We're not," I say. "We came to look for our friend. Can we help you with that?"

I take a carton of waters and start arranging them in a similar manner as her.

"Thanks."

Blade steps over to the literature table and pretends to examine the brochures.

"This is such a beautiful and peaceful place," I say.

She nods. "It's perfect for what we do."

"How long have you been here?" I ask. "Were you here last week?"

"We're here all summer," she says. "We get a different group of families every week."

"Our friend was here last week," I say. "Maybe you saw her. We don't know why she was here. She does this sometimes . . .

goes off her meds and disappears on us, but she's never been gone this long before."

I pull the picture of Charlotte out and show her.

She takes it and studies it.

Nodding, she says, "I believe I saw her, but can't be sure. See so many people each week."

"Did she attend any of your activities or did you just see her on campus?"

She closes her eyes and scrunches her face. Eventually, she shakes her head and opens her eyes. "Just not sure. Sorry."

She hands me the picture. I put it away and we both return to arranging the bottles of water onto the tables.

"Do you happen to know what other groups were here last week?" I ask.

"Let's see . . . There was a singles group, some kind of corporate retreat, some Methodist youth groups from Ohio, a writers' conference, a grief recovery group, a women's conference, and a pre-marital counseling conference. I may be forgetting some. Last week was busy."

"Sounds like it."

"I always try to interact with the other groups as much as possible. No telling how many of them have cancer within their extended families."

"Do you recall if she was with anyone or by herself?" I ask.

She closes her eyes and scrunches up her face again. "Seems like she was with a man around her age, maybe a little older, but . . . I could be completely wrong about that. I just can't be sure. So many people."

"Sure. I understand. And I appreciate your help."

"If I'm thinking about the right person," she says. "She seemed very upset and either was or had been crying."

CHAPTER
TWELVE

FOR THE NEXT several hours we wander around the campus asking questions and flashing the photo.

We get further confirmation about the groups that were here last week, but can find no one who was here with any of them—apart from Marcy Ditmore.

And we can't find any other workers who remember seeing her or are willing to say so.

As the sun is setting we find ourselves seated on a wooden bench beneath a massive old oak tree in a canopied green with a view of the river.

"So," Blade says, "she was either here for a singles meetup, a corporate retreat, a Methodist youth group camp, a writers' conference, a grief recovery group, a women's conference, or a pre-marital counseling conference."

"Or," I add, "none of the above."

"Probably wasn't at the youth camp or the writers' conference," she says.

"She's been full of other surprises," I say. "Maybe she's working on an epic novel or has a kid who lives in Ohio and came over here to see her or him."

"We don't know shit," she says with a sigh. "This was a wasted trip."

We fall silent and I lean back and look up at the thick ancient spreading oak limbs and the excessive amounts of Spanish Moss draped over and hanging from them.

Small birds flitter around them as squirrels scramble along the tops of the branches.

A red-winged blackbird, which are plentiful here, swoops down and lands on the outstretched arm of a Jesus statue, its glossy black feathers and scarlet and yellow shoulder patch shining in the gloaming.

I then look past the oaks surrounding the green down to the river and the setting sun beyond.

From some unseen place on the campus chimes begin to ring out.

I recognize the tune as an old hymn of some sort but have no idea what it is.

"Sure is peaceful and beautiful here," I say.

"Not enough to make the trip worth it," she says. "Colossal waste of time we don't have."

I don't say anything and sit in silence for a few moments longer.

The headlights of the vehicles on the causeway begin to blink on as evening eases into night.

"You want to talk about Dimitri or—"

"No," she says.

"It would help."

"Help what?"

"You," I say. "To process what happened. No matter how evil he was or how warranted what you did was . . . it was a traumatic experience and—"

"Not for me it wasn't," she says. "His ass the one got traumatized. Should be talkin' to him."

"Okay," I say, lifting my hands in surrender. "But if you ever want to talk about it or anything else I'm here."

"I know you are. But I'm good."

"I know you're tough as blue twisted steel," I say, "but I worry about . . . what it cost you to be that way."

"Worry about something else, brah," she says. "I'm legit okay. Must be far enough along on the sociopathy spectrum that cuttin' up thievin', rapin', murderin' bitches don't cost me sleep or anything else."

"Still do you good to talk about it," I say, "so if you ever want to . . ."

Her phone rings and she pulls it out of her pocket.

"Need to take this," she says and jumps up and walks away.

I check my phone again to see if I've missed a call or message from Pete. Finding nothing, I stand and walk down toward the river.

Standing near a row of tall planted palm trees I gaze out at the darkening waters snaking around the marsh grass, and I feel a sense of calm and peace that is rare for me.

What is it I wonder?

Being still. Being quiet. And doing both of those things enveloped in such tranquil beauty. Or maybe it's something else.

I'm not sure what it is but I'm grateful for it, and I'm still trying to cling to it when Blade walks up and says, "Got a surprise for you."

CHAPTER
THIRTEEN

WE FIND a place to change clothes and freshen up and with the road mostly washed off us, she drives us back across the causeway and into downtown Brunswick.

"Does this have anything to do with Charlotte's disappearance?" I ask.

"Nope. This is about us needing a night off and some fun. You do remember how to have that, don't you?"

"Not so much, no," I say. "Not lately anyway."

"Well, welcome to your refresher course."

We drive down Newcastle St. in the downtown district, find a parking place, and get out.

"First," she says, "we're having dinner here."

Here, is a storefront restaurant called Reid's Apothecary, located in one of the many old buildings that line Newcastle.

Inside the fine casual dining establishment she gives the hostess her name and says, "I have the password too."

"You won't need that until a little later," the hostess says.

She leads us to a table in the back corner that gives us a view of the entire dining area and bar and, through the windows, part of Newcastle.

The menu, which is impressive, says that Reid's Apothecary

serves thoughtful plates and handcrafted cocktails, providing a daily dose of fresh, local remedies to nourish the mind, body and soul.

"This is on me," she says. "Get whatever you want."

"Wow," I say. "Thank you."

I have a Georgia peach salad made of spinach, honey roasted pine nuts, cherry tomatos, fried goat cheese, and with warm bacon vinaigrette.

Blade has the grilled steak salad with balsamic vinaigrette.

We then have a bowl of tomato bisque with smoked gouda and garlic buttered crostini.

For her entree she has grilled Australian lamb, summer vegetable risotto with a mint demi glace.

I have the crab cakes with cajun remoulade, yellow saffron rice, and sea island peas.

"This is so nice," I say. "Thank you so much for this."

"Feels good to act like normal human beings occasionally, doesn't it?" she says. "Wouldn't want to make a habit out of it or nothin', but . . . now and then's not bad."

"What's up with the password?" I ask.

"You'll see. Just enjoy your dinner and get ready for dessert."

For dessert we have funnel cake fries topped with caramel and chocolate sauce sprinkled with powered sugar.

When we finish dinner and have our final cocktail she says, "Now it's time for the password. But I have to get something out of the car first."

She pays and I thank her again.

Outside, she says, "Wait for me by that alleyway right there. Won't be but a minute."

I walk over to a long alleyway formed between two old buildings. It's brightly but softly lit by strings of globe lights hanging above it.

On the brick wall of the building to my left a faded white rectangle has stenciled letters that read VOTE AGAINST PROHIBITION @thestudyatreids.

When Blade returns she's carrying my guitar case.

"Please tell me you didn't convert that into an El Mariachi gun case," I say.

"Follow me," she says and hands me the case.

She leads me down the alley way into a dark parking lot and then into a door in the back of the Reid's building.

We walk down a long, dim hallway to a door on the right side.

She taps on the door.

A bouncer in black opens it and steps out. "Do you have the password?"

"Chicago Lightening," she says.

"Welcome," he says, stepping aside. "Come on in."

We enter a literary themed speakeasy called the Study. A youngish female keyboardist and young male drummer are playing on a stage to our left. The bar is in the back directly in front of us, and scattered throughout the large open room are couches and highjack reading chairs and cocktail tables.

The joint is warm and decorated for Christmas. It's crowded and loud, filled with a diverse crowd having a nice time.

We walk to the bar along the back wall and order drinks.

The bartender is a thin, dark complected woman with black eyes and straight black hair who appears to be Native-American.

The dim, well stocked bar is lit by a suspended beam from the high ceiling with a strand of large string lights wrapped around it.

A sign next to the bar reads, CLOSED FOR VIOLATION OF NATIONAL PROHIBITION ACT BY ORDER OF THE UNITED STATES DISTRICT COURT.

After giving us our drinks, Blade's credit card and receipts are handed to her in a hardback book with the dust jacket removed.

"Cool place," I say. "Nice vibe. How'd you find it?"

"I have my ways."

I glance back at the stage. The keyboardist is killing it.

"She's very good," I say.

She nods. "And check out those gams."

She's lit from beneath by a greenish spotlight shining up from the stage that mostly lights her long, shapely, muscular legs. She's wearing a skirt and high platform shoes, both of which show off her stunning legs as they move about keeping the beat and stomping on the sustain pedal.

As she finishes "Favorite Mistake" by Sheryl Crow and receives an enthusiastic ovation, she says, "Thank you. We're gonna take a short break, but we'll be back in a few and will be here 'til midnight, so stick around. And . . . we have a very special treat for you tonight. While we're on break Lucas Burke all the way from Panama City Beach, Florida, is going to play for us."

I turn to Blade. "I am?"

"You is," she says. "Surprise."

"Give him a hand," the keyboardist says as she stands up. "Come on up."

I make my way over to the stage.

"Y'all sound incredible," I say. "So good."

"Thanks, man," she says. "It's his first night playing with me. He's keepin' up pretty well, don't you think?"

"Y'all are tight. Sounds like you've been playing together for years."

"The stage is yours," she says. "Do whatever you like—for about fifteen or twenty minutes."

The drummer says, "You want me to sit in with you?"

"I'd love that," I say.

"Cool."

I pull out my guitar, throw the strap on it, quickly tune, and plug in.

"I appreciate y'all havin' me tonight," I say. "Love the vibe of this place and downtown Brunswick in general. I'm gonna do a few originals for you and then get this amazing band back up here."

I start strumming and go through the chord progression twice. On the second time through the drummer joins me. He's good and adds a lot to the song. He's got a nice touch and doesn't try to do too much.

I play three originals of the confessional singer-songwriter variety and realize this crowd wants to rock. If anyone is listening to what I'm doing I can't tell.

I've played for people who weren't listening plenty of times before. This time I do what I've done every other time before. Focus on the song and the performance and play as if it's a listening room environment instead of a bar filled with talky-talkies and give it my all.

"Nice tunes," the keyboardist says to me when she comes back up. "Love your lyrics." Into the mic she says, "Give it up for Lucas Burke. Love your sound, man. That was nice."

When I find Blade she's chattin' up a tall blonde with green eyes and a mouth full of large bright white teeth.

"That was great," the blonde says. "You're great. You wrote those?"

"Blade says, "Cindy, Burke. Burke, Cindy."

"Thank you," I say. "Nice to meet you." Turning back to Blade I say, "I'm gonna stick this in the car. Be right back."

She nods but her attention is back on the blonde.

The bouncer lets me out and I walk around to the front through the alleyway and lock my guitar in the car. When I get back inside the Study, Blade and the blonde are gone.

CHAPTER
FOURTEEN

I GRAB the only open seat at the bar and order another drink.

When the bartender brings me my drink, I show her the photo of Charlotte and say, "She didn't happen to come in here last week, did she?"

She looks at the picture and shakes her head. "Don't think so."

"Thanks."

"You lose her?"

"She's missing," I say. "My partner and I have been hired to find her. Make sure she's okay."

"I didn't work every night. Might check with the bartender in front—in the restaurant. She was back here a couple of nights last week."

"Thanks."

"I liked your songs," she says. "Thought-provoking. Cool sound."

"Didn't think anyone was listening," I say.

"I was."

"Appreciate that."

I sip on my drink and look around some more, checking out the diverse crowd.

Julie is doing a soulful, mournful cover of "Fast Car."

I still haven't heard from Pete and wonder if Lexi is still alive. Of course, you couldn't really call the state she has been in lately alive. I check my phone. No messages from Pete or Blade.

When I finish my drink, I walk out back around the side to the front and enter Reid's Apothecary.

The bartender is a thickish white girl with enormous breasts, short black hair and plenty of black ink on pale skin.

"Hello, handsome," she says, "what can I get you?"

"Vodka cranberry, please," I say.

"Comin' up. Where you from?"

"Panama City, Florida," I say.

"Oh, cool," she says. "Used to go there as a kid. What was the name of that little amusement park?"

"Miracle Strip," I say.

"Yeah. I loved that place. And the water park . . ."

"Shipwreck Island," I say. "It's still there. The beach is built up and mostly unrecognizable, but it's still there."

"Shame," she says. "The bastards keep paving paradise and putting up a parking lot."

"Where Miracle Strip was is literally a parking lot now," I say. "It's heartbreaking."

She places the drink in front of me on a cocktail napkin and stands there waiting for my reaction.

I take a sip and nod. "That's perfect. Thank you."

"Sure, sugar. Don't have much else going. Closing up soon. You should go to the Study in the back."

"Just came from there," I say.

"Oh, you want food? Kitchen's closing soon."

"The bartender back there said you worked in there a few nights last week," I say.

"Yeah?"

"Did you see this woman?"

I pull out the photo of Charlotte and place it on the bar between us facing her.

As I do, I think again how she reminds me of someone.

She looks at it and starts shaking her head. "Not in the Study. But she was in here. Came in for lunch on . . . Wednesday maybe."

"Was she with anyone?"

She nods. "Older woman. Had some resemblance. Maybe her mom. Or an aunt. Or . . . could just be a coincidence."

"Don't suppose you overheard any of the conversation."

She shakes her head.

"Did it seem like they were upset or having conflict or drama or—"

"No, just quiet conversation with their meal."

"Have you ever seen either of them before or since?"

She shakes her head again. "Sorry."

"What about their server?" I ask. "Maybe they overheard something?"

"Not here tonight and wouldn't speak to you anyway. Just the way he is. Old school. Would never repeat anything over-heard by patrons at his table."

"Okay," I say. "Thanks for your help. I really appreciate it."

I go return to the Study in the back and look for Blade. She's still not here. I text her but don't get an immediate response.

I start to order another drink and sit and listen to the excellent music, but decide instead to leave.

Wanting to be alone, I head back up to Newcastle to walk around the empty sidewalks of downtown.

It's a cool night. The air is thin and easy to breath.

Fronting the old buildings of downtown Brunswick are hexagon-patterned sidewalks, old fashioned street lamps, and a tree-lined median. Most of the shops have Christmas decorations and lights, and the wreaths and strings of lights on the trees and light poles add a festive feel to the revitalized business district.

Plenty of cars are parked along the street, their noses angled in toward the businesses, but the sidewalks and streets are empty, only the occasional passing pedestrian or vehicle.

I pull out my phone to FaceTime with Alana again but see that's it too late.

I haven't walked far when I see a little strip joint across the way called the Red Carpet Lounge.

It's tucked away on a side street and has been in business for over fifty years.

Wondering if Destiny made an appearance there while she was here, I cross the street and walk down to it.

The bouncer, who is standing out front, is a large white man in biker attire, including a black leather jacket with an Indian Motor Cycles logo on it.

I speak to him as I walk up and he nods and gives me a sort of low growl.

"My name's Lucas Burke. I'm from Panama City. I'm looking for a missing woman who was here last week. She's a dancer at Cloud Nine there and I wonder if she came in here or even performed while she was here."

I pull out the picture and offer it to him.

He glances at but doesn't take it.

Shaking his head, he says, "She hasn't been here."

"Would you tell me if she had been?"

He shrugs.

"There's a Bay County Sheriff's investigator who will vouch for me," I say. "I can give you his number."

"No need. She hasn't been here."

"Okay. Thanks."

I turn and start to walk away.

"You don't want to come in for some titties?" he says.

"Not tonight," I say. "Thanks, though."

I cross the street and walk a few blocks before coming to a little park called Machen Square.

Beneath the canopy of a magnolia tree a flowing fountain is surrounded by wooden benches. I enter the park and take a seat on one.

It feels good to be in the peaceful silence. It feels good to be alone.

And before long my heavy eyelids close and I doze off.

CHAPTER
FIFTEEN

MY RINGING PHONE rouses me to consciousness.

My head has been tilted back on the top of the bench at an extreme angle and hurts as I lift it.

Rubbing my neck I reach in my pocket for my phone.

It's Pete.

"How's it going over there?" he asks.

"We've confirmed she was here," I say. "But not much more than that. And we already knew that."

"Well, whatever she got up to over there probably has nothin' to do with her disappearance," he says. "That's part of the reason I'm callin'. But the other reason you'll want to hear first."

"Okay."

"Finally got word back about Lexi," he says.

"And?"

"They did take her off the ventilator," he says.

My heart sinks and I nod to myself as he confirms the news I have been expecting.

Someone behind me says something and I turn toward the voice.

An elderly black man in rags and a raincoat with longish thick fingernails says, "Can I bum a smoke?"

"Sorry," I say, standing to face him. "Don't smoke."

"No problem, my man," he says.

"You hungry?" I say. "There's a food truck behind Reid's. I can get you—"

"Not hungry. Just lookin' for a smoke."

He moves on down the dim sidewalk and I return to my conversation with Pete.

"You okay?" he asks.

"Yeah," I say.

Realizing, how stupid it was to fall asleep in the park, I remain standing and move to a different position so that the large tree is behind me and I can see anyone approaching.

"So, anyway, they unplugged the machine . . . and she started breathing on her own. They're warning the family not to read too much into that, but it is . . . it's better than . . . It means there's still hope."

Relief spreads over me.

"You there?"

"Yeah," I say, my voice hoarse with emotion. "Just . . . relieved to hear that."

"I'm happy for you," he says.

"Thanks, man," I say. "And I heard what you said about the doctors warning. I get it. But for now I'm just glad there's at least some hope left."

"Sure."

"What was the other thing you called about?"

"We've got further confirmation that Charlotte did make it back over here and was here a few days before she vanished, so . . . unless someone followed her from there . . . or something . . . whatever happened to her probably has nothing to do with her trip over there. So y'all come on home."

CHAPTER
SIXTEEN

"TRIP WASN'T A TOTAL WASTE," Blade is saying through a yawn.

I know what she means, but I say, "Oh, yeah?"

"*Oh, yeah.* Cindy was hella fun. The things that girl can and will do with her tongue . . ."

"Nice," I say.

It's the next morning and we're driving back home.

We're both a little sleep deprived and keep yawning.

As it got later and later last night and I still hadn't heard from her I had gotten in the car, locked the doors, reclined the seat, and tried to get some sleep.

Cindy had dropped Blade off at the car at just before daylight this morning and we decided to drive back then.

"You think Charlotte was having lunch with her mom?" she says. "If she lives there she shouldn't be hard to find. Let me see what I can do."

She pulls out her phone and begins tapping and sliding her fingers across the screen.

I call Pete.

"Anyone update on Lexi?" I ask.

"No, sorry, man," he says. "I'll let you know the second I hear anything at all."

"Thanks. Who's listed as next of kin for Charlotte? Any mention of a mother or aunt living in Brunswick?"

"Hold on, let me get back to my desk. Y'all headed back?"

"Yep yep."

"Do you think you found a family member over there?"

"She was seen having lunch with an older woman who bore some resemblance."

"Gotcha. No. We got nothin'. No next of kin listed."

"Okay. Thanks. See you soon."

As I hang up with Pete, Blade says, "Got nothin'."

"Just because they met in Brunswick doesn't mean she's from there," I say.

"True. But . . . I'm beginning to think that Charlotte may just be another alias."

"Would tell us something if it is," I say.

"Bitch is deep in hiding," Blade says.

"Find out from who we might find out where she is—or who has her."

"I left her picture with Cindy," she says. "She's a manager at Reid's and very connected. She'll let us know what she finds out or if the older woman is spotted again."

"Cool," I say, and begin talking about other aspects of the case until I hear her snoring.

CHAPTER
SEVENTEEN

THAT EVENING I MEET DECLAN, one of the bouncers, and Rachel, the house mom, of Cloud Nine at the Craft Bar at Pier Park.

We're at a high table in the back of the large, open room not far from the kitchen. The long bar that runs the length of the left wall is full, as are most of the tables filling the rest of the space. Conversations and laughter join the sounds of drinking and eating and serving, ricocheting off the hard surfaces of the concrete floor, faux brick walls, and wooden bar and tabletops.

According to its menu the Craft Bar is a gastropub.

I'm unfamiliar with that term so pull out my phone and look it up.

A gastropub is a pub that serves food of a similar quality to a restaurant. The term was coined in the 1990s in the UK.

The unfortunate and off-putting term is derived from gastronomy and was coined when David Eyre and Mike Belben took over The Eagle pub in Clerkenwell, London, and converted the British pub, which was known as a drinking establishment with little emphasis on the food, that was served into a joint known as much for its food as its drinks.

The Craft Bar says it serves craft beer, hand crafted cocktails, and chef-inspired food--all with a focus on local and regional sources.

Both Declan and Rachel have raved about the food here and I look forward to trying it.

Miss Rachel, as she's known by the dancers at Cloud Nine, is a large white woman with a pretty, pale face, hair dyed a bright red, and an enormously ample bosom.

She's genuinely sweet and kind, and though she's not much older than the girls who work at Cloud Nine, she has a mature maternal nature many of them lack.

Declan is a large, muscular black man nearly as wide as he is tall.

Rachel and Declan are a couple.

"We always go to dinner before we go to work," Declan is saying.

"And this is one of our favorite places," Rachel adds.

"Brah, I'm tellin' you," Declan says, "they have the best collard greens you've ever tasted in your life. You like greens, don't you?"

"Of course."

The waitress, a petite young woman with deeply tanned skin and black hair up in a ponytail, comes over with our menus and silverware.

"We know what we want," Declan says, handing the menus back to her. "We'll order while he figures out what he wants."

As I study the menu, they order some of those hand-crafted cocktails the menu bragged about and enough food for six people.

"You know what you want yet?" the waitress asks me when they're done.

"I'd like the Nashville Hot Chicken and the braised greens," I say. "And can I get some ranch with that."

"What would you like to drink?"

"Could I get a hand-crafted half-and-half tea, please?"

She laughs.

"And do you have cornbread?" I ask.

She nods. "We do."

"Could I get some cornbread with the greens, please?"

"You sure can, sweetie."

"Becks," Declan says to her, "you been holdin' out on us. How come we ain't know y'al had cornbread? Hook us up with some of that too."

"You got it. Sorry, I thought y'all knew."

"Oh, you thought we knew you had cornbread and we just didn't want any?"

"Well, when you put it like that . . ."

She saunters away from the table and they look at me.

Rachel says, "I can't believe we have another girl missin' from the club."

"I can," Declan says. "It's a dangerous gig. Number of creeps that come up in there on a nightly basis . . ."

"I recognize the other one—what was her name?" Rachel says.

"Nora Henri," I say.

"Yeah. Nora. I realize she didn't work there, but still . . . she came by looking for work the night she disappeared."

A few months back Blade and I had worked the case of a young mother and her baby visiting Panama City Beach who vanished after leaving a truly bizarre 911 call. She had stopped by and talked to Rachel about possibly working at Cloud Nine the night she disappeared.

Declan looks at me. "You ain't surprised Destiny went missin', are you?"

I shake my head. "Unfortunately . . . not in the least."

He looks at Rachel. "Now you see why I keep your fine ass back in the dressin' room 'stead of out front where the sick boys are."

"I do," she says. "Thank you, baby."

Becks brings our drinks.

I fish out the lemon wedge in my tea and place it on my napkin.

They lift their cocktails and I hold up my tea.

Declan says, "To a long life and a fun one, A quick ending and a happy one, A good girl and a pretty one, a strong drink and another one."

"Cheers," Rachel says.

"Salut," I say.

We chink our glasses, tap the table with them, and drink.

"How's that hand-crafted tea?" Rachel asks.

"Not as good as these cocktails," Declan says. "Promise you that."

"It's very gastro," I say.

"Yeah," Declan says. "They coulda done without that in the name, but . . . the drinks and food make up for it."

"So," I say, "any ideas where Destiny might be?"

"Shallow grave be my guess," Declan says.

"God, I hope not," Rachel says.

"Barrel at the bottom of the Gulf," he says. "If she's lucky."

"*Lucky?*" Rachel says.

"She could be in some sadistic prick's dungeon room bein' raped and tortured on the regular."

"Oh, my God," Rachel says. "Please, no."

"She have any run-ins with management?" I ask.

Rachel shakes her head. "She kept her head down and just did her work. Kept to herself."

"We all know who eighty-sixed her ass," Declan says.

"Owens?" I say.

"Logan motherfuckin' Owens," he says.

"How often did he come in the club?"

"A lot at first," Rachel says. "Like when they were courting."

"Courting?" Declan says. "Courting at a strip club."

"You know what I mean."

"I do, but it wasn't courting."

"But after they got together and were seein' each other outside the club he stopped coming in," she says.

"I was surprised he let her keep strippin' when they got together," I say.

Declan says, "It was part of his kink. Even when he did come in he'd just sit in the corner and watch her work the other guys."

"The Owens I know likes to be more hands-on," I say.

"Oh, he was hands-on when they left the club," he says.

Rachel says, "She didn't say a lot, but what she did say was disturbing. He liked to hurt her. He'd choke her. Hit her. Fist her. He'd punish her for what she did with the others guys at the club."

"Why didn't you tell me that?" Declan asks.

"'Cause it didn't happen at the club and I didn't need you goin' to prison like he did for messin' with Logan."

"Another thing I don't understand is why he was into her in the first place," I say. "He's always liked underage girls."

"Yeah," Declan says. "It was strange."

Our food arrives and we dig in.

The Nashville Hot chicken is tender and just the right amount of hot and, as Declan promised, the greens are the best I've ever had.

I look up what braising means because I've never had any green or vegetable taste this good.

According to Google braised means to heat slowly with oil and moisture in a tightly sealed vessel. It's a combination of covered roasting and steaming.

But that doesn't explain the flavor, which is rich and delicious and has a bit of a kick.

"I have to say . . ." Rachel says, "There was more to Destiny than there seemed. She was . . . more complicated, more . . . she seemed like different women at different times. And I'm not sure any one knew the real her."

"We're finding that out."

Declan sings, "Just 'cause she dance the go-go don't make her a ho, no."

"I spoke to Crystal about her—or I did until we were interrupted by a Russian and y'all had to step in and save my ass. Any other dancers or staff I should talk to?"

They both nod and she says, "There's a new shooter girl she spent a good bit of time with."

Declan says, "Her boyfriend hits her and Destiny was tryin' to help her, support her, but get her to leave."

Rachel says, "Her real name is Brandy Haines."

"Boyfriend's name is Len Jennings," Declan adds.

Rachel adds, "Maybe he found out what Destiny was doing and . . . did something to her."

I nod. "We'll check him out. Any customers pay particular attention to her?"

He nods. "She had a few fanboys."

"More like OnlyFanBoys," Rachel says.

"She had a few regulars," he says, "but two more regular than the rest. One's a sweet old dude been comin' to the club for years. He sort of goes from girl to girl but stays with them a long time. His latest was Destiny. He was good to her and she was sweet to him. He'd come in a few nights a week—more recently —and buy up most of her time. She'd sit with him for most of her shift. They'd go back to VIP a few times throughout the night. He probably gave her a grand a night. Like I say . . . he been doin' this with different girls for years. Don't think any of them have disappeared."

"What's his name?"

"Gerald. I'll get his info for you, but go easy on him. I don't think he had anything to do with anything. Now the other fanboy . . . Can't say the same about his creep little ass."

Rachel says, "Rayden Payne."

"Yep," Declan says. "He like the exact opposite of Gerald. He just started coming to the club 'cause he just turned twenty-one.

Destiny was like his first love and shit. His little ass fell hard too."

"He's obsessed with her," Rachel says. "She told me she could handle it and seemed to be, but . . . that was in the club."

Declan adds, "Got no idea what goes on outside the club. I'd start with him."

CHAPTER
EIGHTEEN

BRANDY HAINES IS A PALE, fluffy, early-twenties young woman who dresses to accentuate her large breasts, sloping belly, bubble butt, and thick thighs, and I am unable to tell if the too-small tank top and shorts she has on are pajamas or clothes.

Beneath a mountain of blonde hair extensions, she has over-sized blue eyes and a round, full face with copious amounts of makeup. Her painted face expertly conceals a bruised, puffy right eye and a swollen upper lip.

Later that night, I find her at the Trash Market in an alley in St. Andrews.

The popup market of folding tables and canopy tents is for items made from repurposed and recycled materials.

Artistic images are being projected on the side of the Native Store building, soft, gentle music emanates from an unseen PA system, and a young girl wearing multi-colored fairy wings dances on a wooden box near a dumpster.

The vibe of the market is chill—peaceful and quiet and low-key.

Brandy's booth consists of three folding tables forming a U that she's seated in the center of. The tables are filled with draw-ings and paintings on the surfaces of discarded household items

—random dishes, pots, pans, records, books, empty wine bottles, shoe boxes, toys, and the like.

"I really like your work," I say.

"Thanks," she says, giving me a quick glance then looking away. "Let me know if you have any questions."

"I have questions," I say.

"Fire away," she says with another quick glance that sort of scans past my eyes.

"They're actually related to your other work," I say.

"Oh," she says, and doesn't look up.

"I'm a PI. I've been hired to find Destiny. Did you know she was missing?"

"Oh," she says again and seems a little relieved. "Ah, yeah. Well, I wasn't sure. I knew she had her wedding and honeymoon coming up. Girls sort of come and go in there anyway. So . . . but I did hear someone say they thought she just sort of vanished."

"Someone mentioned you two were pretty close," I say.

She shrugs. "I mean . . . can't really be too close with anyone in there, but . . . I was probably as close to her as anyone there. I don't know."

"You're pretty new there, aren't you?"

"Yeah."

"Was she helping you figure things out?"

"Yeah, I guess."

She's still looking down, busying herself with rearranging the items on her table.

"Was she worried about anything?" I ask. "Anybody bothering her or . . ."

She shrugs. "There's always . . . I don't know . . . issues with certain guys. But . . . nothin' out of the ordinary."

"Did she tell you about her trip to St. Simon's Island last week? Do you know why she went?"

"Said she just needed to get away for a few days."

"Did you see her when she got back?"

She nods. "Yeah. We worked a couple of nights together at the end of last week."

"How'd she seem?"

"Just . . . like she always did. Just sort of normal. Normal for her I mean. I'm not sayin' there's a normal that everyone acts like."

"Nothing happened on her trip to upset her or make her scared or—"

"Not that she mentioned. She was . . . she acted just like always."

"Did she talk to you about her fiancé Logan Owens?"

"Not really. Didn't talk about herself much at all. Mostly just about me."

"What about you?"

She looks up and around, her eyes skimming past mine. "She was like a big sister or a young, cool mom. She cared about me. Was worried about me."

"About your boyfriend?" I ask.

She looks back at me, her eyes locking onto mine for the first time.

"What about him?" she asks, pain in her eyes, fear in her voice.

"The way he treats you," I say. "Him hitting you."

"How—How do you know that?"

"Did she try to get you to leave him? Did he know?"

"He didn't have anything to do with what happened to her," she says. "You need to go. I'm working."

"I'll go," I say. "I'm sorry I upset you. But . . . know this. He won't stop. Guys like that never do. Destiny was right. Your only play is to leave him. When you're ready my partner and I can help."

I take a card out of my pocket and hand it to her.

"We can help you get away from him and protect you."

Her eyes glisten and she blinks back and wipes at tears. "Please go," she says. "Please."

CHAPTER
NINETEEN

"THE FUCK'S YOUR PROBLEM?"

I'm walking to my car on a dark side street when a large muscular, heavily tattooed man who I assume is Len Jennings, Brandy's abusive boyfriend, steps out of the shadows and onto the sidewalk in front of me.

"Based on your demeanor I'd say at the moment you are."

"You're damn right I am. What did you say to her?"

"To who?" I ask.

"You know damn well who," he says. "Brandy. You made her cry."

"Who?"

"My—"

"Punching bag?" I offer.

"What'd you say?" he asks, his voice rising as he takes a step toward me.

He smells of sweat and testosterone.

"I said the only kind of man worse than one who hits women is one who abuses children, but it's close."

"I'm about to hit you, you little bitch," he says. "And keep on hitting you until you don't have a face no more. What did you say to her?"

"Look," I say. "Listen. I know you spend a lot of time in the gym and the tattoo parlor and think you're a badass. And I know you're used to beating up on people smaller than you, especially women. And obviously you're bigger and more muscular than me, but . . . know this . . . I'm a professional. I deal with guys like you all the time. And more importantly I was raised in the system and have rage issues. Look at me. Look in my eyes. Do you see any fear?"

He looks away.

"If the fisticuffs start," I say, "I won't stop. You'll have to kill me or at least render me unconscious. Look at me. Look in my eyes. Am I lying?"

He tries to make eye contact but can only hold my stare for a moment.

"I'm a PI working a case of a missing woman," I say. "The cops are involved. They and my partner know where I am. They know about you."

"I ain't wantin' no trouble," he says, backing down. "I just don't want you upsetting my girl."

"Nothing I or anyone else could say to her could be a fraction as upsetting as being punched by you."

"I've never punched her," he says.

"This missing woman," I say. "Danced under the name Destiny. Was she trying to get her to leave you? Did you make her disappear to get her to stop?"

"What? No. No way. I—"

"You're here threatening me after one brief conversation with Brandy," I say. "Did you try to scare Destiny off and she would't scare? Did she fight back? Things get out of hand?"

"Man, you're crazy. I did't make nobody disappear. Just leave me and my girl alone."

He turns to walk away.

I feel dismissed and disrespected. I had been readying myself for a fight. I'm all keyed up, adrenaline coursing through me, every nerve jangling.

"How about *you* leave your girl alone?" I say. "Get some counseling. Get into a program. Get some help. You can't want to be the kind of weak, pathetic, insecure guy who hits women."

He shakes his head and and keeps walking.

Deep in the basement of my being the pilot light of the furnace of my rage ignites with a glowing poof.

"Len," I say. "You're on our radar now. Not only as a suspect in Destiny's disappearance but for domestic abuse. We'll be watching you. I strongly recommend you don't lay another hand on her."

He keeps walking. Gives no reaction to what I've said.

Something about the carefree way he's walking and the casual way he's ignoring me really gets to me.

I can feel myself starting to lose it.

"You better respond," I say.

When he laughs I'm no longer in control of myself.

I run up behind him and swing my fist as hard as I can, bringing the base of it down hard onto the back of his head.

His knees buckle and he crumbles to the concrete.

Jumping onto him I continue to punch and hit and slap and beat him. Until his face his bloody. Until my hands are sore and aching. Until I'm gasping for breath.

When I come to my senses again, my swollen knuckles bruised and blood covered, I realize I have just beaten a man after telling him how wrong he was to beat his girlfriend.

CHAPTER
TWENTY

"YOU DID WHAT?" Blade is saying.

"I know," I say with a disgusted frown and regretful shake of my head.

We are in an older strip mall shopping center on 23rd Street parked in front of PC PC Repair. PC PC Repair is short for Panama City Personal Computer Repair but only using the initials makes the repetition seem like a mistake.

"If he reports it you're back in prison."

"I know."

Behind us, 23rd is congested, bumper to bumper vehicles accelerating and decelerating, stopping and starting, on their way to work or shop or play or whatever else normal people do.

"Don't get me wrong . . . his ass needed beatin'," she says. "You should'a just let me do it."

"You weren't around."

"What, I can't have a life 'cause I gotta be with you twenty-four-seven on the off chance somebody need their ass beat?"

"People we deal with . . ." I say. "It's not really just an off chance. More often than not they need their ass beat."

"True, but I gotta have some time to get laid and brush my teeth and shit from time to time."

"You're the one who brought up babysitting me in case there's a need for a beating. Wasn't my idea."

"You just got to stop actin' like a fuckin' roid head."

"I'm working on it."

"Apparently not hard enough. I don't want to see your ass sent back to prison."

"Not as much as my ass don't want to be sent back to prison. Guarantee you that."

"Then get your shit together."

"I'm working on it."

"Work harder."

"I will."

"And smarter. Work harder *and* smarter."

"I will."

"Bet. Okay, we ready to go in?"

Without waiting for a response, she opens the door and bolts up out of the car. I follow.

Inside the computer repair shop we find a long, mostly empty space with folding tables filled with repaired and refurbished computers leading to a service counter in the back with a cash register on it.

Behind the counter is the man-child we've come to see.

Rayden Payne, Destiny's young OnlyFanBoy, is so small and slight he looks more like a child than a twenty-something. He has short blond hair, parted on the side and swooped over in the front, and pale blue eyes so light they seem nearly colorless.

He's dressed in khakis, brown slip-on shoes that match his belt, and a tucked-in red PC PC Repair sports shirt. Even with all three buttons of his shirt buttoned his narrow neck leaves plenty of space inside his collar.

His PC PC Repair name badge reads Ray P.

Behind him is a curtained backroom which is where I'm guessing the repairs take place, but for all I know could be a dungeon where Destiny is being held captive, and unless she or someone else is back there, he's the only one beside us in the shop.

"Welcome to PC PC Repair," he says in a soft voice. "How can I help you? Y'all lookin' to buy a new system?"

"What makes you say that?" I ask.

"Oh, well, you're not carrying a computer. Most people comin' in for a repair come in with a computer in hand."

"Do you only repair PC's? Blade asks.

He nods. "Yes, ma'am."

"And only in PC?" I ask.

He pauses a moment, confused by the question, then studies me to see if I'm fuckin' with him.

Letting out a little awkward laugh he says, "Yes. Only here in Panama City. Y'all looking for a gaming system or something to run a business with or—"

"We're lookin' for Destiny," I say.

"I'm not familiar with that brand, but I know we don't carry it."

"Destiny the dancer," Blade says.

"The one who gets your hard drive going," I say.

Blade shakes her head. "Bet this little boy model doesn't come equipped with a hard drive. My guess is a little Microsoft is about the best he can manage."

"What?" he says, his voice tight and high. "Who? What?"

"Destiny," I say. "Your girlfriend experience. Where is she?"

Sweat pops out on his forehead and he places his small hands on the counter top to stabilize himself. "I . . . I don't know."

"She in the back?" Blade asks.

"Pay no attention to the stripper behind the curtain," I say in my best Oz voice.

"What? No. I . . . I don't know where she is. I would . . . I could never hurt her. Or anyone."

"Mind if I take a little look back there?" Blade asks as she walks around the counter.

"Sure. Help yourself. I'll show you—"

"You stay out here with me," I say.

Blade disappears behind the curtain.

"Tell me about your relationship with Destiny."

"I didn't have a relationship with her," he says.

"Didn't?" I ask.

"Yeah?"

"Why use the past tense?"

"She's not at Cloud Nine anymore."

"Where is she?"

"I don't know," he says. "I thought . . . I know her wedding was coming up. And she had a trip or something. Figured she was done with dancing. I was sad I didn't get to say goodbye to her. She was just . . . She was really sweet to me. I liked her a lot. I miss her."

"Ever see her outside of Cloud Nine?"

He shakes his head. "Well, not socially. One time I saw her at Publix and one time she brought her computer in for me to fix, but . . . that's it."

"Any idea where she is?" I ask.

"No. None. Is she okay? Did something happen?"

"That's what we're going to find out," I say.

"I hope she's okay."

Blade comes through the curtain and back around to join me in front of the counter, shaking her head when I shoot her a quizzical look.

"If you had anything to do with her disappearance," I say, "tell us now so we can help you out of the mess you're in."

"I didn't. I would never."

"If you know anything about it," Blade says, "you better tell us now."

"I don't," he says. "I swear. I . . . I love her. I would never do anything to hurt her—or let anyone else do anything to her. If I can help . . . you . . . find her or anything. If I can help with her computer or anything . . . anything at all. Let me know."

CHAPTER
TWENTY-ONE

GERALD POWERS ISN'T what I expected.

He meets us at Caffe del Mundo in the Cove and shows up on a 1966 Harley Davidson Sprint. The vintage bike is all gleaming black and chrome with the one exception of the red shocks.

He's wearing a wife beater, black leather pants, black biker boots, large mirrored shades, and a matte black Germans skull cap helmet. He's tall and thin and has longish gray hair slicked back.

He notices us admiring his bike as he takes off his helmet and shades.

"She's a beauty, ain't she? I've owned her since she came out and the only one to ever ride her. This model is actually a hybrid of America's Harley Davidson and Italy's Aermacchi. Got a 250cc horizontal four-stroke single. It's basically an upgrade, more evolved version of the '61."

We nod. Blade more enthusiastically than me.

"She's a sweet little thing," Blade says.

"You ride?" he asks.

"Every chance I get."

"Groovy," he says. "Y'all hungry? I'm starvin'. Let's go in and grab some grub."

Caffe Del Mundo, which means coffee of the world, is owned and operated by Jimy and Marta Thorpe, and is located in an old laundry mat on Bonita Avenue in the Cove.

It features a full espresso bar, tea, smoothies, an extensive wine collection, and a variety of sandwiches, bagels, and the like.

It's a very tranquil environment, perfect for us to interview Gerald.

Gerald orders a white chocolate strawberry espresso with almond milk and a chicken salad sandwich. I have Sangria and a cuban. Blade has a grilled cheese and a Coke.

We sit at a table in the back near the stage.

"I hope like hell y'all find her," Gerald says. "I've done some looking around myself and haven't come up with anything. She's like *gone* gone."

"Where did you look?" I ask.

"Her place for starters."

So he knows where she lives.

"Anything stand out?"

"I didn't go in. Just looked around the complex. Spoke to her neighbors. Came up with exactly nothin'."

"How did you know where she lived?" I ask. "Had you been there before?"

"Yeah. She was having some issues with her drain and I took a look at it for her."

"So," Blade says, "not just a cool biker dude but a handyman."

"Bit of a Jack of all trades."

"Is that the only time you went there?" I ask.

He shakes his head. "Went back for dinner a few days later— sort of a thank you for fixing her drain."

Caffe del Mundo is a dog friendly establishment, and several patrons have come with their dogs in tow. A small man with a large labradoodle sits at the bar not far from a large woman with a small mutt.

"Wonder why she didn't just let the apartment complex maintenance department handle it," I say.

"Said she didn't want them in her place. She'd had trouble with one of them in the past."

"Do you know who?"

"They only have two," he says. "It was the fat one."

"What'd he do?" Blade asks.

"Not sure exactly. Think it was the way he looked at her and some comments he made. She said he smelled real bad too."

Behind the bar, Jimy is firing up the roaster, dumping the beans into the double-barrel machine. Within a few minutes the first crack occurs and it sounds like popcorn popping.

"Mind tellin' us about your relationship with Destiny," I say.

"She was a sweetheart," he says. "A little older than a lot of the girls. No drama. Smart. Great conversationalist. We spent a lot of time together."

"In and outside of the club?" I ask.

He gives a little shrug and nod. "Yeah, but mostly in. We went to dinner a few times. That sort of thing. We talked so much we really got to know each other."

I wonder if that's true or if she was just playing a part and who he really got to know well doesn't exist.

"I'm a lonely old man and I hang out at Cloud Nine a lot. I've spent time with a lot of the girls there over the years. Charlotte was different."

So she told him her real name. Or he found it out some other way.

"She was . . . She wasn't always on the make. She wasn't running a game or pretending to be into me to separate me from my money. She was chill. We mostly just hung out and talked. We'd go back in VIP occasionally, but even that was different than with any of the other girls."

"How so?" I ask.

"Well, in just about every way. She didn't belong there—working as a stripper I mean. No drugs. No drama. No daddy issues. No money problems. And she was smart."

I think about the Destiny I met and interacted with on a few occasions and how she seemed nothing like the woman he's describing.

"No ideas where she could be?" Blade asks. "Places we should check. People we should talk to."

He sighs. "I wish I did. I feel so bad for her. I hope she just decided to leave her life and start fresh somewhere else, but . . . I know that's . . . not very . . . I know that's probably not what happened."

"Did you give her large sums of cash?" I ask. "Could she have saved enough cash to disappear?"

"Strippin' is a cash business," he says. "She could've saved up quite a bit."

I nod and think about that.

"Look, I realize y'all have to investigate me—especially because of what happened to Indigo, but . . . do it as quickly as you can and move onto real suspects, 'cause I didn't have anything to do with what happened to her."

"Indigo?" Blade says.

"The other dancer who went missing," he says. "I was her main customer too. It was about two years ago at a different club—the Dollhouse. I figured y'all already knew. Guess I just made myself look more suspicious, but . . . the lifestyle most of these girls live . . . and the work they do . . . puts them at risk, but I didn't have anything to do with that one either."

CHAPTER
TWENTY-TWO

ON OUR WAY back to Charlotte's apartment complex to talk to Silas Segal, the fat maintenance man who Gerald Powers said creeped her, I call Pete and put him on speaker phone.

"Indigo Fontenot," I say.

"Yeah?"

"Another dancer who went missing about two years ago."

"Really? Let me pull it up. Oh, yeah. From the Dollhouse. Missing Person report filed by a Gerald Powers. Says he was a fan of hers from the club. But she wasn't really missing she just moved back home. Lots of transient girls work in places like that."

"Where was home?" I ask.

"Cincinnati."

"And y'all confirmed that's where she was?" I say.

"Says investigator spoke with the missing girl's mother and she reported that Indigo was in fact headed home."

"That's it?" I ask. "Headed home?"

"Yep. Guess he figured she'd reach out if her daughter didn't show up."

"Wow."

"It's obvious the investigator didn't believe she was missing and was just humoring the old man. She was an adult. She could do what she wanted."

"You satisfied with that?" I ask.

"I would've done a little more," he says. "Wouldn't have taken much more time or effort."

"Can we get the mother's name and number from you?" I ask.

"I'll text it to you."

"Thanks, Pete. Let us know when you're free for a meal. We owe you."

"I ain't buyin' any of it," Blade says.

"Any of what?"

"Any of any of it," she says. "Not a word the Nerd Squad said—"

"Oh, Rayden."

"And not a word Biker Granddad said. Nor any of this bull-shit about this girl just going home."

"So young, but oh so cynical," I say. "But I agree. Your cyni-cism is warranted."

"Warranted as fuck," she says. "Let's see what Fat Silas has to say for himself."

CHAPTER
TWENTY-THREE

WE FIND Silas Segal in the maintenance shed of Sunset Palms, Charlotte's apartment complex.

It's a smallish building in the back with a view of the much touted olympic size swimming pool, poolside veranda, and fireplace and grill area—all of which are empty on this cold, gray day.

He's a huge man in a navy-blue uniform and matching cap.

Unkempt hair curls out beneath the soiled cap and his reddened face is in need of a shave. The shirt of his uniform is partially untucked, his work boots are untied, and his name tag is missing.

"You Fat Silas?" Blade asks.

He shakes his huge head as he turns toward us. "No. Just Silas."

"From what we hear your big ass gonna be *Inmate* Silas before long."

He shakes his big head again. "Not likely. Who are you?"

"We the PIs who gonna find the missing woman."

"Well," he says, gesturing expansively to the work shed. "She ain't here."

"So you know who I'm talkin' about?"

He nods.

"We hear you gave her a creepy vibe."

"No."

"That wasn't a question. It is what we heard."

"Well, you heard wrong. I ain't done nothin' to that lady or anyone else. I just do my job. I work hard. Keep this place runnin'."

"You got a master key to all the apartments?" she says. "You sneak in and steal dirty panties and dildos. 'Cause we heard a lot of those go missin' around here."

His face reddens even more and he can't hold her gaze. She's scored a direct hit.

"I don't steal and I don't mess with anybody and I don't know where that lady is."

"Did she catch you creepin' her place?" she says. "She freak out and you were just tryin' to keep her quiet, calm her down? You didn't mean for any of this to happen, did you?"

"No. Nothin' happened."

"Silas," I say. "We've got security footage of you entering her apartment."

"I enter all the apartments. And I've never been in one without a work order. Never."

"What's goin' on here?"

We turn to see an older Mexican man with a thick salt and pepper mustache in the same uniform Silas is wearing.

"They're askin' questions about that nice lady who went missin'," Silas says.

"No they aren't. Y'all need to leave right now or I'm callin' the cops. You can't come in here harassing our employees."

"We just—"

"No," he says, pulling out his phone and beginning to tap in a number. "Not another word. Leave now. Last chance. I'm sick of Silas gettin' picked on. He's a good man. Hard worker. Wouldn't harm a fly."

When we don't move, he presses another button on his

phone. "Yes," he says into it. "2141 Sunset Palms Way. We're in the Maintenance Building in the back. There are two individuals harassing and agitating my coworker.

"You can hang up," Blade says. "We're leaving."

As we walk away, he says into the phone, "Never mind. They're leaving. But I'd like to remain on the line with you to make sure they really go."

CHAPTER
TWENTY-FOUR

THAT NIGHT while Blade stakes out Silas Segal, I keep Alana.

Ashlynn, Alana's mom, is on a date with a guy an online service set her up with and is sending me text updates on how it's going.

As usual, Alana and I play a series of games she makes up, many of which are inspired by the Youtube videos she watches.

We are chased by scary purple creatures. We must dive onto the couch as the floor beneath us becomes lava. She is Sonic the Hedgehog and I am Dr. Eggman.

Next we pull out the construction paper, scissors, markers, and the small misshapen bottle of Elmer's Glue and make art projects at the kitchen table—the kitchen table that is already covered with colorful marks, flecks of glitter, and nicks from scissors mishaps.

"I wish you could keep me all the time," she says.

"I'll try to adjust my schedule so I can keep you more."

"Your what?"

"Schedule. It means the order you do the things you have to do."

"Do I have a shedool?"

"You do. You had us play pretend games first, then do the art projects, and whatever you choose next will also be part of your schedule."

She nods and continues concentrating on her drawing.

"What would you like to do next?" I ask.

She shrugs. "I don't know."

"What about writing a letter to Santa?" I ask. "Do you know what you want this year?"

"Yes, I want a Sonic blanket and watch and costume and a Bluey House and a—"

"When we finish our art, I'll help you write all that down for Santa."

"Okay."

As much as I try to be fully present when I'm with her, I feel my mind drifting to other things. I wonder if Lexi is still alive. I wonder how Blade is getting along with Silas. How Ashlynn's date is going, which makes me dread the day she gets involved with someone and brings them into Alana's life.

I check my phone for updates.

"What're you doin'?" she asks. "Stay off your phone. Color your picture."

"I was just checking to see if your mom had texted."

As I check the text I see Pete's again and decide to attempt to call Paula Fontenot, Indigo's mother.

"I need to make a quick call," I say. "It won't take but a minute, then I'll finish my drawing."

"Okay, but hurry."

"I will."

I press Paula Fontenot's number and wait.

It's answered on the third ring by what sounds like an older black man with a deep voice.

"Hi. My name is Lucas Burke. I'm trying to reach Paula Fontenot."

"Haven't heard that name in quite a while," he says.

"Are you her—"

"I'm just the man who got her number after she gave it back,

I guess," he says. "Got a few calls asking for her when I first got it, but that's been quite a while."

"So you know nothing about her or—"

"Nothing at all," he says. "Sorry."

"Sorry to disturb you," I say. "Thank you for your time."

"Not a problem."

As we disconnect, I see a message from Ashlynn. *He's really nice. Such a gentleman. I think he's out of my league.*

No one is out of your league, I type. *No one. Banish that thought from your mind.*

"*Lu-uc,*" Alana says, her sweet little voice exasperated. "It's taking too long."

"Sorry," I say. "I'm done."

While drawing and coloring with my right hand I do a search for Paula Fontenot on my phone in my lap with my left.

My hands are swollen and sore and hurt to use. Earlier in the day I had tried to play my guitar and was unable to without a good deal of pain.

I get a few hits—a couple of Facebook and LinkedIn profiles, but most are too young to be Indigo's mother.

Next I do a search for Indigo Fontenot.

I find an old Facebook account that looks like it could be hers which hasn't been updated since she went missing.

"I can see you," Alana says.

"I'm sorry," I say. "I was tryin' to do one more thing while I was drawing. I'll stop."

"For real this time?" she asks.

"For real."

I place my phone on the table—away from the glue and glitter—and begin working on my picture in earnest.

"Your drawing looks amazing," I say. "You're so creative."

She pauses and looks at mine. "Yours looks good too."

"It doesn't," I say, "and that's okay. I don't have to be good at drawing to enjoy doing it with you."

"You're good at music and playing pretend with me," she says. "And finding people."

"Thank you, sweet girl."

My phone rings.

"*Seriously?*" she says, expressing more disbelief, displeasure, and exasperation in those four syllables than I would've thought possible.

"Sorry. It's Aunt Blade. I'll be quick. I promise."

"Hey," I say.

"I think he's our doer," she says. "He ain't right. Creepy as fuck. He lives in an old mobile home out in the Callaway Heights area. The lot is filled with junk—cars, appliances, and shit—and there's a storage shed on the back of the property. If he goes out I'm gonna take a look around."

"Wait until we can both go in," I say. "Let's do it tomorrow while he's at work."

"She could be in there dying," she says. "He could've decided to get rid of her after we spoke to him today. If he leaves I'm going in."

"I'll join you when Ashlynn gets back. Keep me posted."

"Anything on your end?"

"Paula Fontenot's number doesn't belong to her any longer and I can't find anything current on her or Indigo online."

"Shit," she says. "If she's missin' and they're connected it means it's Gerald not Silas, but . . . I'm tellin' you . . . Silas ain't right."

"That's not quick, Luc," Alana says.

"Got to go," I say to Blade. "Keep me posted and don't do anything stupid."

CHAPTER
TWENTY-FIVE

ASHLYNN'S DATE goes extremely well. When she returns home she is actually giddy.

She tells me about it in code after Alana gives her a recap of our evening and shows off her artwork.

As they head to bed, I get ready to go join Blade, but as I'm about to open the door to leave, she and Pete walk through it.

"I was just headed out to join you," I say.

"He went to bed. Pretty sure he's in for the night. We need to have a little come-to-Jesus meeting with Law and Order here."

We each grab a drink and drop into chairs around the kitchen table.

"Any updates on Lexi?" I ask Pete.

He frowns and shakes his head. "Sorry."

"I want to go in," Blade says. "In the morning when he goes to work."

Pete says, "You go in illegally and we can't use anything you find. He'll walk. Tell her Luc, It can't just be about finding the missing woman. We've got to put away the doer. Or he'll keep doin' it."

Blade says, "We don't work for the sheriff."

"I know," he says. "You work for a criminal. But don't turn into criminals."

Blade makes a cat noise and raises her hands like claws. "That's pretty low, bro. You know why we workin' for the particular criminal element we workin' for."

"Sorry," Pete says. "I didn't mean it like—I meant if you break into his place you're committing a crime. And no matter what you find—and let's just say you find the worst thing imaginable—he'll walk. He won't go down for any of it. It'll all be fruit of the poisonous tree."

The pale skin of Pete's face is etched with the fine lines of fatigue and purplish half-moons hang beneath his eyes. He's probably not only tired from a long day, but of having this conversation with us.

"She could be in there," Blade says. "Tied up in that shed. Still alive but barely, the clock ticking."

"She could be," he says. "Or she might not be. She could already be in a shallow grave somewhere and not by Silas's hands. The old dude could've done her and Indigo. Or it could be the Russians from the club or whoever pulled a gun on Burke at KLS. We just don't know yet. But if you break in and—"

"Our job is to find her," she says. "That's it. Not to build a winnable case in court against whoever has her."

"Your job has to be more than that," he says. "That's just your first priority and I get it. But you're acting like she's alive and finding her while she still is is all that matters. But what if she's dead. You find her dead body, but because of the way you find it . . . the killer walks."

"If I find her body in there I'll back out and the sheriff's office will get an anonymous tip."

"Everybody knows y'all are working the case," he says. "It'll come back to y'all. And to me."

"Is that what this is about?" she says. "You saving your job?"

"No. Of course not. I can't believe you can't see that there's a right way to do things."

"We disagree about what that is," she says. "Your way, the legal way, is not necessarily the right way."

"It *is* for catching and putting away monsters. It's not the fastest or easiest, but it is the best way to secure a conviction. But you're right for finding someone who's missing without worrying about making sure whoever took them can't do it again, your way is much faster. The thing is . . . we only have each other. We have to look out for each other 'cause nobody else is. That's all I'm tryin' to do."

"And we appreciate it," I say.

Pete says to Blade, "This isn't like you. Usually you're more . . ."

"I got caught up," she says. "I just had such a strong feeling that he's a sick creepy fuck and has her in there."

He nods. "I get it. I do. And I appreciate it. I'd feel the same way. We all would. But this is just about the best way to bring the perp to justice. There's something else."

He pauses.

"Must be important with an ominous pause like that," she says.

"You two have some notoriety," he says. "Y'all done some great work. But it has put you in the spotlight. And you're getting a reputation. You're right on the edge. If the sheriff finds out you broke into Silas's or anyone's place . . . you'll not only lose your license, but you'll be brought up on criminal charges. And not just B and E, but obstruction . . . and that carries some serious time."

I say, "We're sorry for the position we've put you in. You're always so good to help us and—"

"I like to," he says. "I really appreciate all y'all are able to do."

"We've relied on you so much and we haven't really realized the extent to which your connection to us causes you issues with your boss and coworkers."

"We all want the same thing," Pete says. "Help the exploited and bring justice to predators."

He's right, and I realize that he's motivated for many of the same reasons we are—abuse we suffered in childhood.

I nod. "But we go about it in slightly different ways. And I think there's a need and a place for both approaches. You're right that we have to do things within certain parameters or we won't be able to do them anymore. But . . . think about my experience with . . . the so-called justice system. I went to prison and Owens didn't."

"And I'm tryin' to prevent anything like that from happening again. That's what I'm tryin' to say. With y'all more visible and with you on probation . . ."

"We more vulnerable," Blade says. "More exposed."

"Speaking of Owens . . ." Pete says. "I meant to tell you . . . The girl you saved from him . . . She died a while back. She had moved away and changed her name and—"

He continues talking but I don't hear what he's saying. I feel like I've just been sucker punched and I'm unable to breathe.

I had gone to prison and lost track of her. She wanted a fresh start with anonymity and I had respected her wishes and hadn't looked for her. Maybe I should have.

"You okay?" he says.

"'Course he ain't okay," Blade says.

"Sorry," Pete says. "I just figured you'd want to know. I didn't think about how—"

"How'd she die?" I ask.

"Overdose. It's unclear whether it was intentional or accidental."

"Didn't save her from him after all," I say.

"I'm sorry I didn't . . ." Pete says. "Y'all know sometimes I say things the wrong way. I had been meaning to tell you and . . . we didn't find out until just recently, but . . . my mind was on— I'm worried about what y'all might do and . . . I'm sorry I just said it like that."

"It was gonna land hard no matter how it was said," I say.

"But—"

"I need some air," I say. "Gonna go for a walk."

CHAPTER
TWENTY-SIX

THE COLD AIR FEELS GOOD, but the Christmas lights and decorations do nothing for my mood.

I walk fast then begin to jog, as if trying to outrun how I'm feeling.

It doesn't work, of course.

Eventually I stop running and start walking again.

My heavy breaths come out in puffs of fog in the cold night air.

I call Heather.

"Are you okay?" she asks. "What's wrong? Why are you out of breath?"

"I just feel like everything is so fuckin' futile," I say. "All I do or try to . . . comes to nothin'. All I do is spin my wheels, waste my time. I'm not helpin' anybody. I'm not savin' anybody."

"I'm sorry," she says. "So, so sorry it feels that way."

"Doesn't just feel that way," I say. "That's the way it is."

"Okay."

Her unwillingness to argue the point drains the fight right out of me.

"All I did," I say. "All I've been through. All it cost me. All it's still costing me. And for what? He's still free, still out here doin' whatever the fuck he wants and she's dead."

"Who's dead?" she asks. "Charlotte? Lexi? Who?"

"Carrie."

"Who?"

"Carrie Davis. The underage girl Logan Owens was drugging and raping. The one I caught him with and beat him so bad it put him in the hospital and me in prison. I thought we saved her, but . . ."

"What happened?"

"She killed herself," I say. "Well, he killed her . . . just took a while for her to die."

"It just happened?"

"I just found out about it. Happened a few months back."

"Oh, Luc, I'm so sorry."

"She really was such a sweet innocent girl," I say. "He started drugging her without her knowing it. She came to Panama City Beach with a group of girlfriends for spring break. Met him and he . . . pretended to be something he wasn't. She disappeared. Her friends didn't tell her mom until they had to—until they got back to Atlanta without her. By that time she had been missing for nearly a week. Her mom and sister contacted the police and they opened a missing persons case. After a few weeks of getting nowhere, her mom hired us to find her. We did. Owens had her the whole time. Got her so strung out she didn't know her name. The things he did to her . . . the state she was in . . . the . . . what he was doing to her when we found them . . . I wanted to kill him . . . and almost did."

I think back to what Pete has just been saying about our different approaches and realize that if we hadn't broken into Owen's place and I hadn't lost it and beaten him to within an inch of his life he might be in prison now and not causing other girls to vanish and making me his errand boy. Pete could've used that to win his argument, but didn't.

"Pete's right," I say.

"Huh?"

"Nothin'. Didn't mean to say that out loud. Was just thinking about something Pete said."

"What can I do?" she says. "How can I help you? Want to come over? Want me to come to you?"

"Just talking to you helped. Thank you. I've got to go."

"You sure? I'm worried about you. I'd really like to see you. To check on you."

"I'm okay. And I appreciate you. Thank you. Let's get together when things slow down."

"But they never do," she says.

"They will. I promise."

"Before you go . . ." she says.

"Yeah?"

"I know you don't feel like it and there's nothing I can say to change how you're feeling right now, but . . . you are making a difference. You are saving people. Finding lost souls. Reuniting them with their loved ones. I'm so sorry for what happened to Carrie. It's truly tragic. But when you can . . . think about all those you have saved. And remember that you gave her a real chance. If it was too late for her by the time you found her . . . that's not on you. Put that blame on who it belongs to."

Even as she says it I know I'm going to kill Logan Owens.

CHAPTER
TWENTY-SEVEN

THE NEXT MORNING as we're driving out to Silas Segal's property in the Callaway Heights area, I call Pete.

He had been gone when I got back last night, and I have things I need to say to him.

"Morning," I say. "How are you this morning?"

"I'm good," he says. "Got some information for you."

"Before we get to that there's something I want to say to you."

"Okay," he says, his voice becoming a little guarded.

"I wanted to thank you again for what you said last night and the way you said it. When I was walking I realized that what you were telling us, because you care for us, was exactly what we needed to hear. I also thought about how Owens walked because we broke into his place and because of what I did to him. I know that's what you were trying to tell us. You could've used that as an example but you didn't. I'm sure that's what made you think of his victim dying. Anyway, I just wanted to say you were right and I appreciate you lookin' out for us."

"Thanks, Luc. I appreciate that. I do care about y'all and want y'all to be okay and to get to keep doin' what you're doing."

"Okay," Blade says, "before y'all start singing Kumbaya or some shit tell us what you got for us."

"It'll just confirm what you already know," he says, "but KLS is a dummy corporation. It's a front for several other companies. It was set up internationally by an attorney out of Birmingham. So we have no idea who's really behind it, but I can tell you this . . . based on their activities and other companies . . . I'd say they're a security company."

"So like us?" Blade says.

"No. Nothing like y'all. Think Blackwater. We're talkin' mercenaries with government contracts operating all over the world. Very dangerous dudes who are used to operating with impunity."

"And a stripper dating Logan Owens worked for them," Blade says.

"We've got to talk to Keisha Barjon again," I say.

"I'd say stay away from her and KLS," Pete says. "You're not going to get anything out of them and they may dismantle your life just for trying. I'm serious. You've never dealt with people like this before. They're not just extremely dangerous . . . they're well connected. We're talkin' an army of mercs all over the world with their Uncle Sam's permission to do whatever they want to. The biggest, best PI firm in the country would be no match for them and y'all . . ."

"Ain't that," Blade says.

CHAPTER
TWENTY-EIGHT

SILAS SEGAL'S blue-roofed single wide is on a wooded lot off of a dirt road east of Callaway. Nearly every foot of it is covered with rusting junk—vehicles, engines, appliances, lawn-mowers, and tires. It sits in the center of a heavily-wooded pine flats forests so there are no neighbors for miles in either direction.

The weathered and flapping blue tarp covering much of the roof is a holdover from Hurricane Michael, the Cat 5 storm that decimated our area.

I shake my head as I look at his place.

"Told ya," Blade says.

The shed she mentioned can't be seen from the road where we are.

"And there's a shed in the back?"

"Uh huh."

"How far back?"

"Fifty feet from the house maybe."

"How'd you see it?"

"Walked through the woods and came up from the back."

I nod and look around some more.

"His truck is gone," she says. "Must already be at work. He drives a little old red Toyota truck."

"We're gonna need more help to set up surveillance on him," I say.

"We ain't gettin' paid for this, remember? We don't have the money for that. Also ain't got that kinda time."

"Well, what do you want to do? You heard Pete. We're playing with our—"

"Just want to take a look around," she says. "Won't touch anything. Won't remove anything. Just take a look around and back out."

"We can't," I say. "Pete was right."

"Tell you what . . . There's windows in the shed. Let's just look through them. Hell, we can almost do it without going on his property. It was too dark last night. Couldn't see anything, but with daylight . . ."

"I think we need to wait," I say. "Watch him more. Follow other leads. Gather more evidence."

"That's a ball sack move," she says. "I ain't talkin' 'bout breakin' in. Just havin' a little look around. Come on."

She gets out of the car and starts walking toward the woods on the right side of Segal's property.

I park the car a little ways down and follow her.

The December trees have long since shed most of their leaves and needles and the understory growth is brown and brittle, but the fallen trees and branches from the hurricane make it challenging to traverse.

When we eventually make it to the back of Segal's yard we find it in much the same cluttered disarray as the front. Two more vehicles, both small trucks, both on blocks, more washer and dryers, more tires, more lumber, tin, and trash.

The portable storage building is natural wood with a green tin roof and a standard exterior door.

We approach the side of the shed, not sure where the property lines are.

"The yard starts there where the grass is," I say, "but the actual property line is probably somewhere out here in the trees. We may already be on his property."

"Well, let's hurry," she says. "Run up there get a quick peek and get out of here."

As we get closer, I can see that the windows to the shed are blacked out.

"We won't be able to see inside," I say, nodding toward them. "But you already knew that."

"Couldn't be sure," she says. "It was dark when I was here last night and I didn't get close."

She continues walking and in a few steps is in Segal's yard.

"Blade," I say. "Let's go."

"I just want to look around a little," she says. "We see a woman's foot print or some other sign she is here . . . then we go in."

"And Silas walks."

"But Charlotte lives."

She takes a few more steps and I reluctantly follow.

"STOP," I yell. "FREEZE."

I do the same.

Another step and she would've stumbled across a tripwire.

As I look around I see a network of tripwires and a series of shallow round impressions about the size of landmines.

"What?" she says.

"Tripwire," I say. "We're—"

"Standing in a boobytrapped minefield," Silas Segal says.

We turn to see him standing behind us with a shotgun. He points to camouflage security cameras high up in few trees.

Time seems to slow down.

My heart starts thumping and I can hear the pounding in my head.

"Know what a Bouncing Betty is?"

I nod. "Heard of them."

"German S-mines that bounce up when triggered and deto-nate about three feet off the ground."

I can feel cold sweat trickling down my back.

"Y'all are surrounded by them," he says.

Every muscle in my body tenses.

"I'm surprised y'all haven't blown up into a million little pieces yet. But I can promise you this . . . take another step or two in any direction I'll be cleanin' you up with a heavy duty shop vac. Still can't believe y'all haven't triggered anything yet. Must've spaced them out a little more than I remember. Been a while since I put them in."

Unbidden a memory from childhood plays like an old film in the theater of my mind.

When Blade and I were living in one of the many children's homes we filtered through as kids, we were taken on a group outing to Miracle Strip, a mom and pop amusement park on Panama City Beach.

The home was always being given free passes to places and other charitable donations. This one was actually a place we wanted to go.

It was a hot summer night in June and the place was packed with sunburned tourists from Alabama and Georgia, but there were plenty of locals as well.

We ate ourselves sick on candied apples and cotton candy and had our small bodies hurled around and jerked up and down on carnival rides like the Bullet, the Abominable Snow-man, Dante's Inferno, and the Music Express.

It was a fun, exciting night—one in which we forgot about our plight for a few hours.

But because as abandoned, unwanted, and orphaned we always had a dark passenger hitching a ride with us, and nothing could ever just be good or light or right. Something sinister, terrible, or horrific always, inevitably had to occur.

Near the end of the night, one of the newer additions to this particular group of system kids, a small boy named Curtis

Mayflowers, climbed out of his cart near the top of the Ferris wheel, up the support frame, out onto the outer rim, and dove to his death.

None of us knew much about him but later found out that one of the older kids was bullying and raping him relentlessly.

What the fall to the asphalt below did to his little body was the most horrific thing I had ever seen until then.

I haven't thought about that for a little while now. Thinking what could happen to me and Blade if we take a step in the wrong direction must have brought that to mind.

Blade says, "Is Charlotte in your shed?"

He shakes his huge head. "No. She ain't. And never has been. I got no clue where she is, so y'all died for nothin'. Next time I'd —Oh, wait. Y'all don't get a next time. Y'all 'bout to vanish like the girl you're lookin' for."

"If you don't have her," I say, "why all the security?"

"Privacy," he says. "It's my right. It's nobody's business what I do."

"It is," I say. "And we don't want to violate it. We're just looking for the missing woman. If she's not here we'll go look somewhere else. Can you tell us how to get out of this minefield?

He shakes his head. "Well, yeah. Just run. Run as fast as you can."

"If you don't have Charlotte and have nothing to do with her disappearance," I say, "the last thing you want to do is commit murder."

"Not murder," he says. "Just standing my ground. Y'all are trespassing on private property. Y'all rather be shot or blown to bits? Me personally I'd like to see you explode."

I turn slightly and slip my hand in my pocket and attempt to pull my phone out without him seeing me.

"Hey," he says. "What do you think you're doing?"

He raises the shotgun and points it at me as he takes a couple of steps in our direction.

"I want to see you get blown the fuck up, but I will shoot you if I have to," he says.

While he's focused on me, Blade slips a knife of some sort out of her back pocket.

Raring back, she throws the knife at him.

Seeing it in time, he steps to the side and ducks and it misses him.

Smiling at his victory he looks back at her but by that time another knife is already on its way.

This one hits him in the upper chest between his shoulder and neck, but like a batter swinging his bat after the ball is already in the catcher's mitt, he attempts a too-late counter maneuver.

And appears to be doing a fat, awkward, out-of-shape rendition of the Matrix move.

As the knife hits him, he screams in pain and drops the shotgun.

Then, as he tries to right himself from his evasive maneuver, he pitches forward and evidently lands on one of his mines because he explodes, bloody bits of him flying in every direction.

The bulk of his torso lands about six feet away. It's missing three of its four limbs and most of its head.

CHAPTER
TWENTY-NINE

"THE HELL'RE Y'ALL DOIN' out here?" Pete asks. "What happened?"

He's outside the perimeter yelling to us.

He's surrounded by several deputies and the Major who's in charge. The sheriff, who was at a meeting in Tallahassee, hasn't arrived yet.

Inside the perimeter, members of Tyndall Air Force Base's Explosive Ordnance Disposal Unit are systematically sweeping for and disarming explosive devices.

Florida's Bureau of Fire, Arson & Explosives Investigations could have been called in, but Tyndall's unit is closer and could get here much quicker.

Both the bureau and Tyndall's EOD are comprised of highly skilled and exceptionally trained technicians who utilize specialized equipment to approach, inspect, disarm and remove all types of explosive devices. And both agencies often assist the Federal Bureau of Investigation and the Bureau of Alcohol, Tobacco, Firearms and Explosives in providing regional counterterrorism training to local first responders.

"We were out on the road where our car is and he came up with a shotgun and forced us to come back here," Blade says.

"Said he wanted to see us explode. When he was about to shoot us, I threw a knife at him and as he fell trying to avoid it he landed on one of his explosives."

If they accept that version of events then we're not trespassing and haven't broken any laws.

The various bomb squad personnel all around us are doing what is known as demining, the process employed to remove land mines from an area. They are using ground penetrating radar in tandem with metal detectors to locate the explosives.

"All these explosives have us wondering what he's hiding in that shed," I say.

"We'll find out soon enough," Pete says.

"Not soon enough for us," Blade says.

"I know, but just hang in there. We'll get y'all out of there as soon as it's safe."

Blade lowers her voice and says to me, "I've already wet myself once and I'm about to have to do it again."

"Me too."

"But I'm really worried about what I'm gonna do when I have to do more than pee."

"Me too."

"Still tryin' to decide what's worse," she says, "gettin blown up or shittin' myself."

I laugh.

We are thirsty and hungry and aching. Our muscles have been so tense for so long that we're exhausted. And our immobility and dehydration is beginning to lead to cramps.

Without moving my feet, I move my body as much as I can—and I see Blade doing the same thing periodically. We've got to shift our weight often and keep our blood flowing well so we don't pass out or seize up. Falling over will most likely lead to a fate similar to Segal's.

"Hey," I say, lowering my voice even more. "Serious talk. If I don't make it . . . take care of Ashlynn and Alana."

"You know I will," she says.

"And . . . just in case . . . I want you to know that you have been the only person on this planet I've been able to count on and I'm so grateful we found each other. You are—"

"Bitch, stop," she says. "I can't be cryin' *and* shittin' myself out here. I know what you sayin'. And the same goes for me. But let's see if we can't survive this shit. Okay?"

CHAPTER
THIRTY

"I WAS THINKIN' about Curtis Mayflowers earlier," I say.

"Of course you were," she says.

"We've been pretty lucky compared to some."

"We've made our own luck," she says. "And we've taken care of each other. And we've had a little help here and there. But that's enough of that kind of talk. I mean it."

"If we do survive," I say. "I think I'm going to kill Logan Owens."

"Now you talkin'," she says. "And just know . . . if you don't survive and I do . . . I'll certainly take care of that for you. Consider that shit done."

One of the technicians inching toward us draws a little closer and says, "The victim didn't land on a Bouncing Betty."

"He ain't the victim," Blade says. "He's the perp."

"Just meant the dude who exploded. There are some Bettys out here, but lots of other devices too. Lots of DIY shit. Good thing he didn't land on a Betty, though. It would've gotten y'all too. They get their name because they bounce up around three feet before detonating. When they do detonate, ball bearings contained inside fly out in all directions. They're lethal at sixty-six feet, but can cause casualties up to four-hundred-and-sixty feet."

"Good to know," Blade says. "I guess."

"Just hang in there. We're workin' as fast as we can, but we've got to be methodical."

"Take all the time you need," Blade says. "Just make sure we don't wind up like ol' Silas over there—and there, and there, and there, and there, and there."

I pull out my phone and look up Bouncing Betty.

It was developed in Germany in the 1930s and used as a defensive strategy of the Third Reich. It's a self-contained anti-personnel mine and was originally named Schrapnellmine or S-Mine. Dubbed the Bouncing Betty by American infantrymen, this deadliest of mines was buried just underground, only exposing three prongs on the top which were usually camouflaged by grass or vegetation.

Because the Schrapnellmine was constructed mostly out of metallic parts, it was easy to detect when metal detectors were employed. But because not enough metal detectors were available, many allied forces had to probe the soil with their knives and bayonets searching for the dangerous mines. When one was discovered, it could be disarmed by inserting a sewing needle in place of its safety pin.

By the time they stopped making them in 1945, Germany had produced over 2 million Bouncing Bettys.

A line at the bottom of the article shocks me and I let out a gasp.

"What?" Blade asks.

"There are still around one-hundred-and-ten-million mines in the ground in the world—and at least that many waiting to be planted or destroyed."

"That's . . . interestin' and all," she says, moving her arms around to indicate the area around us, "but right now I'm just concerned about these ones in this general vicinity right here."

"I'm gonna call Alana and talk to her in case we—"

"Don't finish that sentence," she says. "Just call her. But don't start cryin' and shit. You gotta keep it tight."

"I will."

I wipe my eyes and clear my throat and—

"Bitch, you already—"

"No, I was pulling it together."

"Oh, God."

I pull up Ashlynn on my phone and touch it.

She answers after two rings. "Hey."

"Hey," I say. "How are y'all?"

"All good," she says. "Both a little bored."

"Nice," I say. "Bored sounds good."

"Huh?"

"I just wanted to let you know that Blade and I are in a bit of a situation and . . . we'll probably be fine, but if anything happens . . . Just wanted you to know that I love you and that I have a little life insurance and you are the beneficiary. I wish it was more, but it'll help y'all a little. Stick close to Pete and if you get into any jams reach out to Clyde Brousard."

"What's going on? You're scaring me."

"We'll explain everything in just a little while," I say. "Or Pete will. Can I talk to Alana for a minute?"

"Yeah, but I'm callin' Pete after she gets off the phone with you."

"Luc?" Alana's sweet, soft little voice says.

My eyes sting.

Blade clears her throat and shoots me a pull-your-shit-together look.

"Hey, girl," I say. "How are you? What're you doin'?"

"When will you be home? I'm bored."

"It won't be long," I say. "I can't wait to see you. We'll play anything you want for as long as you want and we'll get ice cream."

"And can I cuss?"

"All you want."

"Hell, yeah," she says. "Well get your ass home and let's play."

"I'll be there as soon as I can. I love you so much sweet girl. And I'm so proud of you. So, so much."

"Hurry home."

"I'll do my best," I say. "Love you. Bye."

"Love you, bye."

We end the call.

In less than two minutes Ashlynn calls back.

"Pete told me what's going on," she says. "Listen to me. Do whatever you have to to stay alive. Okay? We can't . . ."

"We are," I say.

"I have an idea," she says.

"Lay it on me."

"Why not bring in one of those big bucket trucks with the long extension arm like the power company has and have them reach over across the mine field and lift y'all out?"

"That sounds like a great idea to me," I say. "I'll mention it to Pete."

"I already have. Let me know the moment y'all are out and safe."

"Will do," I say. "Love you."

"Love you so much, Lucas. And so does Alana. And we need you. Stay alive."

When we end the call I tell Blade what Ashlynn said.

"That's not bad," she says.

We both turn toward Pete.

He shakes his head. "It's a good idea," he yells, "but there's no way to get a truck like that back in here."

"How about a damn helicopter or some shit like that," Blade yells.

The same tech from before says, "Just hang in there. We're

clearin' a path to get y'all out of here safely. I know it's taking a long time, but we're making sure it's safe. You don't need a truck or a helicopter or anything else. You've got us and that's enough."

CHAPTER
THIRTY-ONE

TURNS OUT THEY WERE ENOUGH.

It took thirteen hours, but Tyndall's Explosive Ordnance Disposal Unit was able to eventually get me and Blade out of Silas's mine field safely.

We are home now, and after showering and hydrating are sitting with Ashlynn and Alana and are extremely grateful to be able to be.

Alana is in my lap playing a game on my phone.

I hold her tightly and hug her often, periodically kissing the top of her head.

As if having sensed something about what might have happened today she's staying even more attached to me than usual.

"When I think of our lives without y'all . . ." Ashlynn says. "I really don't know what we'd do."

"Ain't gonna have to find out," Blade says, stifling a yawn.

"Not today, but . . . how long before y'all are in a similar situation—one that doesn't work out like this one? The work y'all do . . ."

"We'll always be careful," I say. "Always come home to y'all."

"Would y'all ever consider doin' something else?" she asks.

I shrug.

Blade says, "Like what? Ain't nobody payin' to see me strip."

"What if I went back to dancin' and made enough to support us all?"

"That's very, very kind of you to offer," I say, "but . . . we'll be more careful. I promise."

"And it ain't like your job's the safest employment out there itself," Blade says.

She starts to say something, but there's a quick knock at the door followed by Pete letting himself in with his key.

He joins us in the seating area, sinking into the last remaining chair.

"I don't have to tell y'all how close you came to . . . buying it today," he says. "Scared me but good. I'll tell you that. I was so . . . I'm just so glad y'all are still here with us."

"Us, too," Blade says. "Now tell us. Did you find Charlotte?"

He shakes his head. "We found some of her stuff."

"So he did have her?"

"Don't think so. It wasn't like that. His shed was filled with thousands of items belonging to the women of the apartment complex where he worked. Panties. Tons and tons of dirty panties. But all kinds of items, including sex toys and toilet paper and even used tampons. Also had thousands of hours of video footage of them. Upskirt footage. Peeping Tom footage. By the pool. In the workout room. Hidden cameras in showers and toilets. Pretty much anything you can imagine and lots of stuff you can't. But there's no sign that he took Charlotte or ever actually did anything but video and steal their stuff."

"Glad his creepy ass is in pieces," Blade says. "Used tampons. I mean . . .goddamn."

Alana says, "Mommy what's a tampon? And Aunt Blade used a bad word."

"My B," Blade says. "But . . . I was . . . I mean think about what we had just heard. But I'm sorry. I won't do it again."

"We still have a lot to go through," Pete says. "But . . . I don't think he's our guy."

I say, "Any footage of Charlotte that might tell us more about her or show her with any of our suspects?"

"Not yet. But like I say . . . it's going to take a while to go through it all."

"Well," Blade says, "that's one way to mark a suspect off our list."

"There's something else," Pete says. "Segal had security cameras set up around his property."

I know where he's going with this. Been expecting it.

"One of them shows y'all entering his property and him coming later—probably 'cause his cameras alerted him to your presence."

"Oh, yeah?" Blade says.

"It contradicts the statement y'all gave us about him forcing y'all back there at gunpoint."

I nod. "Sorry, Pete. We did the very thing you warned us not to do."

"We weren't gonna break in," Blade says. "We were just having a little look around."

"Somehow," Pete says, "and I have no idea how exactly . . . that footage has been erased. Must have been a corrupted file. Could've been from the explosion. Never know with technology. I don't trust it."

"Thank you, Pete," I say. "And again. Sorry for . . . what we did."

"Right now I'm just so glad y'all are still with us that I'm not even mad."

CHAPTER THIRTY-TWO

WE FIND Keisha Barjon in the parking lot of Publix on 23rd Street loading groceries into her car.

She's dark and diminutive with multi-colored dreads and long, painted nails that come to points like talons. She'd be small in any context, but standing next to her huge black SUV she looks like a child.

She starts shaking her head as we approach her.

"Got nothing to say to y'all," she says.

Her voice is raspy with a hint of Cajun spice in it.

The Publix parking lot is crowded and, like 23rd Street that fronts it, bustling, but she is parked in the farthest spot from the store, presumably to protect her ride, so there are no vehicles or people in our vicinity.

"Why'd you report her missing if you're not willing to help?" I ask.

Instinctually, I begin lifting bags out of the cart and into the back of her car, bending down beneath the open hatch.

"I shouldn't have. It's none of my business and I didn't know . . ."

"Didn't know what?" Blade asks.

"That I'd get so much harassment."

"Who's harassing you?" I ask.

"Y'all."

"This ain't harassment," Blade says. "Nothin' like it."

"We're just tryin' to find your friend," I say.

"She's not my friend."

"Okay. Co-worker. We're just trying to find your co-worker. Don't you want us to?"

She gives a small shrug. "Sure, I guess . . . but . . . I don't know anything and can't help you in any way."

"You know far more than you think," I say. "Even if it's just about her. That kind of background information is what will help us find her. Will you spend a few minutes just answering a few questions?"

"I can't."

"They got to you, didn't they?" I say.

"Who?"

"You know who. KLS."

"No. I just don't know anything and don't want to get involved."

"They scared you, didn't they?"

She looks around and lowers her voice. "They're scary. Probably listening to us right now. Y'all should stay as far away from them as you can."

"You sayin' they don't want her found?" I ask. "They had something to do with her disappearance?"

"Does it sound like I'm sayin' that? 'Cause I ain't. And that's the kind of shit that gets people . . . Don't put words into my mouth. Don't—just leave me alone."

"Look," I say, "we're not tryin' to jam you up. We just want a little info. Just between us. No one will ever know."

She shakes her head.

"Or," I add, "you can talk to the police, which will be much more public and what you say will be leaked to the media. It's up to you, but we're the better option."

"We'll keep you out of it," Blade says.

"Let me ask you a question," I say. "If you were missing and Charlotte could help . . . wouldn't you want her to?"

"Yeah, but . . ."

"Just a few minutes," I say. "Just a few questions."

"Okay, but not here. It's too open."

"Let's get in your vehicle," Blade says.

"*NO*," she says, alarm in her voice. "No. It could be bugged."

"Okay," I say. "Ours."

"I know yours is," she says.

I look around the area. "How about the family bathroom inside the grocery store?"

She nods. "But we can't walk in together. Split up and be discreet."

She starts to reach up for the hatch, but I close it for her. I'm not sure even on her toes she could've reached it.

When she pulls out her keys to lock the vehicle I grab them.

"Just in case you were thinking about driving away when we split up. I'll give them back to you when we finish talkin'."

She shakes her head and gives me a disappointed and disgusted look but then eventually nods.

We each head in different directions and eventually down the parking lot, into the store, and over to the little hallway that leads to the bathrooms.

Waiting until no one is around or watching, we enter the bathroom at different times.

Inside, we stand as far back from each other as we can, which isn't far in the small space, particularly with the sink, toilet, and baby changing station crowding in on us.

Blade says, "This the least sexy time I've ever been in a private bathroom with two other people."

Her words echo around the small room, ricocheting off the hard tile and porcelain surfaces.

"Listen," Keisha says, "I honestly don't know much. I can tell you she's a complicated lady with some real tragedy in her past. She's sad as shit, but she's strong too. Tough. Resil . . ."

"Resilient?" I offer.

She nods. "She's like one of those lizards that can change their skin color. She can be or pretend to be whoever she wants to or needs to or whoever she's with wants her to be or thinks she is."

"That's very helpful," I say. "Thank you."

In the brief pause in conversation the tap can be heard dripping with a fat, wet thump.

"I can tell you that she was up to something," she says. "She asked way too many questions at work—the kind they don't like. She was so curious about how the guys do what they do in the field. Some of the guys thought it was like a come-on, I guess. And I think she slept with a few of them, but she was tryin' to get info. I could tell. Why—I have no idea, but that's what she was doing."

She pauses and I start to say something but then she continues.

"I will tell you this . . . I don't think KLS had anything to do with her disappearance."

"What makes you think that?"

"'Cause they lookin' for her just like y'all are. Now . . . that doesn't mean an individual who works there didn't have something to do with it, but . . . as an organization . . . no. But . . . if someone did . . . take her or hurt her or . . . let KLS deal with it. They'll find out and they'll deal with it."

"What kind of tragedy has she experienced?" I ask.

"Don't know the details, but I think she lost her dad when she was young and maybe a sibling and a spouse later. Again, I'm . . . I don't know any specifics. And I could be wrong about all of it. I'm sure she was playin' a part with me too. But that stuff seemed real. Was said in . . . She seemed genuine and . . . I don't know, unguarded, when she said them."

"Did she—"

"Let me ask y'all something," she says. "Y'all seem like y'all really want to find her—like you really care what happened to her."

"We do," I say.

"That concern just apply to her?"

"Whatta you—"

"Y'all care what happens to me too?"

"We're not going to do anything to put you in a situation," I say. "I promise."

"Really think about that," she says. "She can't be the only one who matters. I matter too. Protect me. Take care of me. Don't burn me to find her. 'Cause that's just trading one girl for another. And that's not—"

"We would never do that," I say. "You're right. That would be . . . We wouldn't do that."

"Swear to me you won't," she says.

"I swear."

She turns to Blade. "You too."

"I swear I won't burn you—not even to find Destiny or Charlotte or whatever her name is."

"Please honor what you're sayin'," she says. "Please keep that promise."

"We will," I say. "You have nothin' to fear from us."

She seems to think about it for a moment, as if considering something, then reaches into her purse, pulls out a thumb drive, and hands it to me.

"What's this?" I ask.

"Video footage of the night she went missing."

CHAPTER
THIRTY-THREE

THE FOOTAGE KEISHA gave us is from KLS cameras located on the high chainlink and razor wire perimeter fence and parking lot.

We are back in our office watching it on our agency laptop.

Blade is seated at our desk. I'm standing beside her, leaning over to get the best view of the relatively small computer screen.

The largely unoccupied industrial park KLS is located in is dark, its parking lots mostly empty. There's very little light and no movement.

Just like when I was there, the building KLS is housed in is dim. The only illumination is a faint glow from a loading dock in the back.

The video also picks up the blink of the security camera lights from the many cameras surrounding the facility.

It's a dark rainy night with very little light. Most of what is visible is from infrared feeds, which have a ghostly, unnatural appearance.

The footage mostly shows the entrance to KLS, its steel rolling gate on a track for vehicles and a smaller electronic gate with a black keypad callbox for pedestrians.

The file we have is an edit from a few different cameras. It begins at 3:01 a.m., about half an hour before Charlotte arrives and shows a man dressed in a long black raincoat and black hat lingering outside the gate of KLS.

Blade says, "Why they lettin' him just hang out like that? Moment you showed up they were all over you."

"He hasn't approached the gate," I say. "And . . . I . . . wonder . . . Maybe he's not technically on their property. He could be just outside of their property line."

"They don't seem like the type that are deterred by pesky little things like property lines."

"True."

"They could know him," she says. "He could be one of them."

"Also true."

"Think he's waitin' for her?"

"He'd have to know she was coming," I say. "And she wasn't scheduled to work that night."

"Maybe she called ahead. Maybe she went to meet him"

"Keisha said she just showed up, but you're right . . . she could've called him directly."

We watch all thirty minutes prior to Charlotte's arrival, during which the man in black just waits. A few times he appears to check his phone, but beside that he just shifts his weight and occasionally moves around a few steps in each direction.

When Charlotte arrives on foot, she crosses the parking lot and makes her way to the gate.

"Something about her reminds me of someone," I say, "but I can't figure out who."

"Seem like a thousand other white girls to me," she says. "So she walks up to the place . . . and we have no idea where her car is."

"Right."

She taps something into the callbox and appears to say something.

As she waits, the man in black moves toward her.

At one point she seems to turn her head in his direction and say something, but I can't be sure.

"Did she say something to him?" Blade asks.

"I can't tell. Maybe. But it's too dark for her to be able to see him. If she heard him walking up or if he said something to her she could've been turning toward him . . . but if she did it was a very, very brief conversation."

A few moments later, Charlotte is buzzed in and the man in black returns to where he had been.

"If they did speak," I say, "KLS security would've heard their exchange. She's right by the callbox."

"If they didn't . . ." she says. "If he didn't say something to her . . . why approach her? And why is KLS lettin' him?"

As Charlotte disappears into KLS, the man in black is the only figure visible on the footage.

We know from what Keisha told us that after entering their workplace, Charlotte had a cup of coffee and talked with Kevin Pendleton, the only employee working that night. She then logged onto her work computer briefly, made a phone call, then, around 4:00 a.m., left.

The footage then shows Charlotte being buzzed through the electronic pedestrian gate and back out into the dark night.

If she has any awareness of the man in black she doesn't show it.

But as she begins to make her way out through the parking lot in the same direction she had entered from he follows her.

Then there's a jump cut to a security camera from a music store in downtown.

It shows a small portion of an empty street and sidewalk.

Then at 4:14 a.m. the footage shows Charlotte walking into and then out of the frame.

Thirty seconds later, the man in black passes through the same frame.

"He's our guy," Blade says. "Followed her to her car and then took her. Who the hell is he?"

We keep watching to see if there is any additional footage but the video ends a few seconds later.

"We need to see if we can get any other footage from downtown that night," I say. "If it hasn't been deleted already."

Blade says, "Wonder why she parked so far away when she could've driven up to KLS and parked in its parking lot."

"Maybe she had been drinking," I say. "Why go to the office at all? Perhaps to sober up. She did drink coffee and just hang out for a little while. We need to talk to her coworker that was there—Kevin Pendleton. See what shape she was in."

"And what he knows about the man in black," she says. "If he was the only one working that night . . . then that's why the man in black got to hang out without being kicked out."

"We need to get a better look at him and try to get an identity. He's either the doer or a prime witness."

CHAPTER
THIRTY-FOUR

KEVIN PENDLETON no longer works for KLS.

Currently he's doing a series of side hustles in an attempt to cobble together a living, including Uber, Shipt, and DoorDash.

Between delivering groceries and restaurant food, he meets us at one of the beach access points along Beach Drive.

Beach Drive runs from downtown to St. Andrews with the Bay on one side and large homes with big bay views on the other. A few places along the road have a few parking spaces and a short, sandy path to the bay.

When we arrive, we find him standing at the water's edge with his shoes off and his jeans rolled up.

He's a stocky twenty-something with sandy blond hair and lightly freckled skin.

The December day is gray, the still bay like slate, and the sand is cold beneath our feet.

It's an odd place to meet, but my guess is if he's as paranoid as Keisha he wants to be somewhere difficult to surveil and where he can see anyone approaching.

"We appreciate you meeting us," I say.

"Not a problem. I just hope you can find Char. Can't believe how bad the police have botched the case."

"Can you tell us about her?" I ask.

"She's good people. A real sweetheart. Always enjoyed talking to her. Very smart. Always asking questions and tryin' to learn."

"About?"

"Everything. She was fascinated by the work KLS does—the techniques, equipment, the dark work."

"Dark work?"

"You know . . . the wet work . . . off the grid, outside the law, usually in other countries. Dark web, dark thirty. She may have just been flattering some of the operatives, but she seemed genuinely interested. I don't know."

"Why'd you leave KLS?" Blade asks.

He looks around and lowers his voice. "Too much testosterone. Organizations like that attract some full-tilt crazy motherfuckers—full of roids and rage and crazy conspiracy theories. Don't get me wrong. They're some decent dudes too, but I just got tired of being around the nuts."

"Do you think any of them had something to do with her disappearance?" I ask.

He shrugs. "Don't have any reason to, but . . . wouldn't put it past some of them. Do that kind of work long enough and you begin to think the rules don't apply to you."

"Any ideas what happened to her?" Blade asks.

He shakes his head. "Wish I did. I miss her. Feel so bad. Never known someone who went missing before."

"Can you tell us about the last time you saw her?" I say.

"It was random. She stopped by the office in the middle of the night. I was the only one working. I was surprised to see her. I knew she had a party to go to that night with her boyfriend."

"She talk about him much?"

He shrugs again. "Some. It's funny. Most of the time it sounded like he repulsed her, like she didn't like him at all. I kept asking her why she didn't break it off with him and she always said she was about to. Just has to do a few things first."

"So she shows up at the office middle of the night," I say.

"Yeah."

"Was she drunk?"

"A little. Not like fall down, but she had a good buzz going for sure."

"How'd she seem?"

"Agitated," he says. "I'm sure it was something he did, but she said she didn't want to talk about it. Just wanted a safe dry place to sober up."

"I made her some coffee. We talked for a little while. I was thankful for the company."

"What was she wearing?" I ask.

"Like a black party dress. She was stunning."

Blade says, "Did you two . . ."

"No. Not really. I . . . we . . . kissed a little, but she said she couldn't."

"Bet that made you mad, didn't it?" Blade says.

"No. Not at all. It was nice—the making out I mean. And . . . I got the feeling that as soon as she finished up a few things and broke it off with her creepy boyfriend we'd . . ."

"So she got you revved up and then slammed the breaks," Blade says. "That's tough."

"No, it wasn't like that. It was tender and sweet. It was . . . just kissing and it was nice."

"What else did y'all do?" I ask.

"She logged onto her computer for a few minutes, but didn't seem to be doin' anything really. Just looking. She went to the bathroom. She called someone but they didn't answer and she didn't leave a message."

"Did she seem scared?"

He shakes his head. "Never saw her scared."

"How sober was she when she left?"

"More than when she came in. She was pretty straight."

"She mention anything about the party or her boyfriend or anyone harassing her or following her or anything?"

"Not really. Nothing I can remember."

"What about the man in black loitering in the parking lot?" I ask.

"You know about him?" he says. "I was by myself. Couldn't really do anything. And most of the time he wasn't technically on our property."

"Did she mention him?" I ask. "Did she see him? Talk to him?"

"I don't know. She didn't say anything."

"Any idea who he is?"

He shakes his head again.

"Is he a KLS employee?" I ask.

He shrugs. "Could be. I just don't know."

"He followed her when she left," I say. "Did you call and warn her or call the police or anything?"

"I . . . I didn't think she was in any danger. I didn't realize he was following her—if he was. The truth is . . . when she left I went to the bathroom."

Blade says, "To relieve some tension built up while she was there?"

He shoots her a look like *you got me.* "I was in there for a little while. I didn't see her or him. Didn't know anything until I looked at the footage after she went missing. I feel terrible. I really do. I hope he didn't have anything to do with her disappearance—not when I could've done something about it."

CHAPTER
THIRTY-FIVE

"ANY UPDATES ON LEXI?" I ask.

Pete frowns and shakes his head. "Last I heard she's still fighting."

I nod. "Thanks."

Pete has just climbed into the backseat of my car with some file folders and a laptop. I'm driving. Blade is in the passenger seat.

We are in the downtown area not far from the industrial park where KLS is located.

"Got some additional footage," he says. "Shows more of the same, but lets us know a little more about her path. She walked down Harrison, crossed 4th, and then up Grace Avenue."

"With the man in black still following her?" I ask.

"Yep yep. He's got to be our guy."

"Wonder why he's following her for so long without doing anything," I say.

"Waiting for the right moment or place or for her to get to her car," Pete says.

"Middle of the night," Blade says. "Downtown's dead. Wonder why she didn't make him."

"Maybe she did," I say. "Maybe that's when he pounced."

Pete says, "Now that we know more about when she vanished and the route she took . . . I've got some additional factors and even a few wild theories."

"Well, two days after the night in question the governor comes for a visit and one of the places he stops is at KLS. Brags on them for providing jobs and helping Florida's great economy —but also for supporting the cause of freedom around the world. Thing is . . . the entire area was swept in prep for his visit, so . . . if the man in black had attacked her or killed her and dumped her body somewhere they would've found her. They searched every manhole, every dumpster, every building, every lot, every everything. Or if her purse or phone or umbrella or anything had been there they would've found it."

"So he follows her to her car and kills or subdues her and then takes her with her things in her car," Blade says. "It's why it's all missing."

"We don't even know if she had her car down here," I say. "She went to a party with Owens. Maybe they rode together."

"We need to know that," Pete says.

"And," Blade adds, "where the party was and more about it."

I pull out my phone and call Clyde Brousard.

When he answers, I give him a little background and let him know what we need to know.

"She drove herself and met him there," he says. "He didn't like it. The party was in one of the old abandoned buildings on Harrison—the one across from the House of Henry where they do all the photo exhibits and art shows."

"What kind of party was it?"

"Two power players—brothers or cousins or something—one was announcing his candidacy for something and the other the start of a new business venture. I think in that same building, but don't know for sure."

"Who can tell us what went on inside that building that night."

"Got a cousin who waited for the caterer. I'll shoot you her contact info and tell her you'll be callin'."

"Thanks. And Owens and Destiny left separately?"

"Yeah. He offered her a ride to her car, but she said she wanted to walk. She told him she'd come by his place a little later, but she never did. I drove him home and he dismissed me. Far as I know he stayed in the rest of the night waiting for her."

"Thanks, man. I really appreciate it."

After disconnecting the call, I tell Blade and Pete what Brousard said.

"So she walks out of the party and over to KLS," Blade says.

"Something could've happened at the party," Pete says. "Angry or jealous boyfriend, husband, wife, whatever. Could've followed her and—"

"The man in black was waiting for her when she got to KLS," I say. "And had been there for half an hour."

"Could've still been at the party."

"True. But if she felt unsafe or threatened by the man in black or anyone . . . wouldn't she have said something to Kevin or just stayed put there where it was safe?"

Pete says, "Must not have perceived the threat."

"Coulda been somebody from the party," Blade says, "but coulda been somebody from the club or from KLS or someone Owens hired—or Owens his damn self."

"So," I say, "we now know where she was before she went to KLS. We know that she had her car down here. We don't know where she parked, but we might be able to find out. We know she had been drinking and was maybe upset about something."

"And because of the security prep for the governor's visit," Pete says, "we know whatever happened to her she nor anything she had with her were left down here."

"But do we?" I ask.

"Whatta you mean?"

"Wonder what the security team does with what they find," I

say. "If they find an umbrella or a phone or a shoe or a purse . . . What do they do with them?"

"That's a good question. I'll find out. I'm also working on getting more footage from down here—or seeing if there is any."

"Do any of the ones you have show the face of the man in black or any other identifiers?"

"I don't think so, but let's look at them again."

He opens the laptop, pulls up the footage, and passes the computer up to me.

I place it on the dashboard and press play.

We all lean in and watch it.

"Not very big, is he?" Blade says.

"Got a pretty distinctive walk too," I say.

He seems to walk up on the balls of his feet, his heels never quite touching the ground. He also leans forward, bending at the waist while keeping his back straight, as if put together with a hinge in his midsection.

"He definitely following her," she says. "Matching her pace."

There isn't much footage and it's poor quality. We watch it a few times, but besides the guy's diminutive size and distinctive walk there's nothing to go on.

I close the laptop and hand it back to Pete.

"Got more to go on now," I say. "And more leads."

"Well, before you start followin' them up," Pete says. "Want to hear my theory?"

"Sure."

"What if someone wanted to assassinate the governor or embarrass him or KLS? What if the guy was tryin' to gain access to KLS? What if he followed her to get the key code or to get her to let him in or somethin' like that?"

I nod. "Certainly sounds like a possibility."

"But it didn't happen," Blade says. "We're pretty sure he got her, but he didn't use her or her knowledge to get into KLS. Nothing happened to the governor or KLS."

"That we know of," he says. "I've got a highway patrol buddy who's on the governor's detail. I'll ask him if anything happened."

"Cool," I say. "And we'll see what Brousard's cousin can tell us about the party."

CHAPTER
THIRTY-SIX

"I AIN'T WANTIN' to get messed up with the *po-lice*," Caden Brousard says. "You feel me, cuz?"

He's a tall, thin young man with long, tapered fingers and fingernails, and a head full of long dreads. His way of acting and talking are part of a performative persona, and as he speaks he repeats certain words so much they've become almost inaudible.

"That works," I say, "'cause we ain't the po-lice."

Blade says, "Ever seen any cops that look like us?"

"Maybe him, definitely not you," he says. "Less you deep undercover or some shit."

He's between bartending gigs at the moment and is working as a cook at the Waffle House in Callaway. He's on a break and we're standing on the cement walkway near the front of the building.

Traffic on Tyndall Parkway streaks by. Across the street, Po Folks and Chick Fil-A are doing a brisker business than Waffle House is, and vehicles are lined up at the drive-through pharmacy at Walgreens.

I say, "Would Cousin Clyde tell you to talk to cops?"

"Nah, brah, he most definitely would not."

"So talk to us," I say. "Won't take but a few minutes of your time and might save someone's life."

"Okay, bruh, it's all good. I just ain't down with the cops."

"Woman at the party went missing later that night," I say. "You remember her?"

"Hell, yeah, I remember her, bruh, she was hot as hell, bruh. Know what I'm sayin', bruh? But she was . . . like all calculated and shit."

"What do you mean?" I ask.

"Not as fake as lot of the rich bitches there, but . . . Or not in the same way. I don't know. You could tell she didn't want to be there but was tryin' not to show it or somethin'. But, bruh, she and her man got into it. Couldn't tell which one was tryin' to tell the other one what to do or if they both were, but they were not havin' a good time. Bruh, I heard him call her cunt, bruh. Straight up. No lie. To her face."

I get so caught up in the way he communicates that all other sounds around us become distant and desultory.

"How did she react?" I ask.

"Didn't hear that. I's passin' by, but a few minutes later she was sayin' somethin' about wantin' to be alone with him. Bruh, she said something 'bout I'll show you what this cunt can do or some freaky shit like that, bruh."

"Did she get into it with anyone else that night?"

"Nah, brah, just her creepy pimp or whatever he is."

"Notice anybody watching her a little too closely or—"

"Bruh, everybody was watchin' her. Can't be that kind of smoke show and act like that and not get noticed."

I start to say something, but he continues.

"There was one dude, bruh. Like an old dude that didn't fit in there. Wasn't like the rest of the . . . Did she . . . Was she a hooker or a stripper or somethin'?"

"Why do you ask that?"

"Old dude acted like and she treated him like a John or a . . . Like a customer or a client or some shit like that."

"How did Owens act toward him or her?"

"Who?"

"Her boyfriend?"

"Like her pimp."

"How'd everyone else act toward him?"

"People were watchin' him too, but in a different way. Sort of sideways. Know what I mean, cuz? Like a freak. You could tell he was used to it and acted like it didn't bother him."

"What about the way he interacted with her?"

"Bruh, I don't know, bruh. Sometimes he seemed mad as fuck, bruh. Other times he was like . . . I don't know . . . amused. At one point I heard her tell him she could fuck whoever he wanted to that she was goin' to. And he said you'll only fuck me and who I tell you to. Or some shit like that. Bruh, it was some fucked up shit."

"How drunk were they?"

He shrugs. "Can't say for sure, cuz. But like . . . some. Think they were trippin' on some other shit too. Not just the wine we were servin'."

"Did they leave together?"

"Nah, brah. She left first. He didn't stay too long after her—maybe five or ten minutes. It was like he was, I don't know, provin' a point or somethin'. Didn't do anything. Just waited. Then left."

We stop talking for a moment as a young couple walk up and enter the restaurant. They look like college students and are holding hands.

When they are inside, Blade says, "Anyone else leave around that time?"

"Not sure, cuz. I's workin' and . . . I mean, I noticed them . . . really her, but everybody else was borin' as fuck. The old man may have. Not sure. Don't remember seein' him again."

"Remember his name?" Blade asks.

He shakes his head. "Never got it."

"Gerald?" I ask. "Powers?"

He shrugs. "Never got it, bruh."

I describe Powers.

He nods. "Sounds like him. Maybe, bruh. Sounds like a lot of old white dudes."

"Didn't happen to be dressed in black, did he?" I ask.

He shrugs. "Yeah, I guess."

"All black?" Blade asks.

"Like biker shit, yeah."

"Did he have a long raincoat?"

"No, idea, bruh. Wasn't coverin' the red carpet. I's steppin' and fetchin' for a bunch of rich white folks."

"Anyone else in all black?" I ask. "Notice any long black raincoats?"

"Bruh, lots of black suits and dresses. Lots of raincoats by the door. That's all I know bruh, and I got to dip."

"Thanks for your help," I say. "We really appreciate it."

"Just make sure I get my cut of that reward money if y'all find her."

After he leaves, I say, "With as much money as Owens has, why hasn't he offered a reward?"

"Because he did it," she says.

I nod.

She adds, "Don't you think Powers is too old and big to be the guy following her?"

"Maybe," I say. "Probably. But it could be the angle of the cameras. Looks far more like Rayden Payne."

"Damn sure do," she says.

CHAPTER
THIRTY-SEVEN

"EVERYTHING I OWN IS BLACK," Gerald Powers is saying. "It's all I ever wear. Why?"

We showed up to his house unannounced and are talking to him on his front porch since he has yet to invite us in.

He lives in a large barndominium on about ten heavily wooded acres north of Panama City off Highway 231.

A barndominium is a sleek farmhouse design that features a large, open concept living space and often horse stables or workshop. In Powers' case it's a massive garage and shop for his many motorcycles.

"Do you have a long black raincoat?" I ask.

"I have a black leather duster," he says. "Why?"

"Did you wear it the night of the party?" Blade says.

"What party?"

"The Smiley Brothers," I say.

"Oh, yeah, I stopped by there. I went to school with their dad. He was a good friend. Didn't stay long."

"Why didn't you mention it when we spoke before?" I say.

"Why would I?"

"You saw Destiny at it."

"So?"

"Then you followed her," Blade says.

"I most certainly did not. I've never *followed* anyone."

"Best we can tell that's the night she went missing," I say.

"Oh. Wow. Okay. But I didn't follow her. I left the party before she did. Her fiancé was bein' a real dick."

"Did y'all get into it?"

"Me and her boyfriend? No."

"What was he doing?" I ask.

"Just the usual. Tryin' to control her. Humiliate her. Embarrass her. She was scared of him. I . . . I know I should've said this before, but . . . I didn't think it was relevant because . . . she's the one missing. Not him. But she was genuinely scared of him. She asked me if I could get her some protection and teach her how to use it."

"What'd you get her?"

"A little slim-line .9mm that could fit in her purse," he says. "I'm only tellin' you 'cause I want you to know how scared she was. She wasn't scared of me. I'm the one she had get it for her and teach her how to use it. She was scared of him. I hope she left him, just vanished in the night, but I bet he did something to her."

"Mind if we have a look around?" I ask.

"My place? Not at all. Got nothing to hide. Just don't wreck the joint."

Though his home is huge, it's so open it doesn't take long for us to search. There are no signs of Charlotte or anything suspicious. He hangs back and allows us to conduct our search, but is close enough for us to ask questions.

"Are there any other structures on the property?" I ask.

"No. Just this one. You're welcome to search the grounds. I just hate for you to waste that kind of time since I know I had nothing to do with it."

"We haven't been able to find any info on Indigo Fontenot," I say.

"I'm just glad you're looking. Somebody needs to."

"The number we have for her mother is no good any longer."

"I seriously doubt their disappearances are connected, but if they're not I'd be happy to hire you to find out what happened to her after you find Charlotte."

"Bet," Blade says.

"Did Charlotte ever mention St. Simon's Island to you?" I ask.

"No," he says. "But . . . that's not that far from Brunswick and Savanah, right? Beautiful place."

"Did she mention Savanah and Brunswick?"

"She didn't mean to, but . . . And I could tell she regretted it after she did, but I think she has some family in that area. I did a bike ride through that region with a buddy of mine about a decade ago. Gorgeous area."

CHAPTER
THIRTY-EIGHT

AS WE'RE WALKING BACK to our car, I say, "Seeing and searching Powers' place reminded me we need to do it for everybody involved. Amateur mistake to only go to Rayden Payne's place of business."

She nods. "He more likely to be the dude on the video than this old fucker here."

"We've got—"

Logan Owen's huge SUV pulls up.

Blade says, "How the hell he know we were here?"

Clyde Brousard puts the vehicle in park, hops out, and walks over to us.

"Mr. Owens would like an update."

Blade says, "I got an update for him."

Broudard tries to suppress a smile. "Not you. Just him."

I nod. "Give us just a moment."

He nods and returns to the vehicle.

"I'm not sure I can be in there with him without throttling him," I say.

"You take him out here and now and one of us gonna have to deal with Brousard," she says. "Be a bitch to clean up. Powers probably be a witness. Best to wait until we can—"

"I'm not sayin' I think this a good time to do it. I'm sayin' I'm not sure I can't. I keep thinking about Carrie. He killed her . . . it just took a while for her to die."

"Tell him we got a lead we need to follow up right now," she says.

I nod.

As I start to walk toward the vehicle she calls after me.

"Whatever you decide," she says. "I'll back your play."

I walk over to Owens' door and wait. Eventually the window rolls down.

"Walk around and get in," he says.

"I can't," I say. "I'm covered in chemicals from a search we just did and we've got a lead we've got to follow up on right now."

"I have to say . . . I thought you would have found her by now."

"We're gettin' close."

"Is she alive?"

"We won't know until we find her. What were y'all fighting about at the Smiley Brothers' Party?"

"The usual. All part of the process."

"The process?"

"Of training her to be a submissive wife."

I clinch my fists down by my sides as my anger and adrenaline spike.

Images of him "training" Carrie seep into my consciousness.

"I've got to go," I say.

"I've decided to hire another agency," he says. "I can't tell if you're not really workin' the case or just this inept, but I've got to find her, to know what happened to her."

"We're going to find her," I say. "Even if you bring someone else in. We're going to find her. We won't stop until we do. We're going to uncover what happened and who's responsible. No matter what and who that is."

"You're of no use to me if you can't complete simple tasks

like this," he says. "I'm going to turn over the evidence to the authorities and put you back in prison where you belong and let someone better at this find her. Last chance. You've got two days."

"We have all the time it takes," I say. "We won't stop until it's done."

Without waiting for a response I turn and walk away.

"Two days," he says above the sounds of his window is rolling up.

CHAPTER
THIRTY-NINE

AS WE'RE DRIVING BACK into town Pete calls.

"Before you ask," he says, "I actually do have a Lexi update. She's still breathing on her own. She hasn't woken up yet, but she's still with us . . . and . . . her vitals are improving slightly."

"Thank you, Pete. That's great news. I really appreciate it."

My phone vibrates with another call. It's from a number I don't recognize and I ignore it.

"Got other news but it's not as great," he says. "I looked through the items that were recovered during the sweep for the governor's visit downtown. The only thing that might possibly be hers is an umbrella that looks like the one she was carrying. Nothing else. No purse or phone or anything."

As soon as the second call ends my phone begins ringing again.

"Supports the theory that she was taken with her things and her car, mostly likely be the man in black."

"But who is he and why'd he do it?"

Blade says, "Not the old geezer."

"Y'all taking Powers off the list?"

"Nobody's off the list," I say, "but he's definitely not the guy in the video and he's about as off the list as you can get and still be on the list."

My phone vibrates a text notification.

I glance at it.

It's from the same number that has been calling.

Answer your phone, it reads. This is Rudyard Pawie, the head of KLS.

"Hey, Pete, the head of KLS is calling. Let me take this. I'll call you back."

When the call comes through again I click over to it.

"Can you and your partner spare me a few moments of your time?" Pawie says.

"Tell us when and where."

"Now. There's an old, empty warehouse off of 231 not far from where you are. I'll text you the address."

When I end the call, Blade says, "How the hell everybody know where we are? I'm sick of this shit."

"I can't see Powers letting them know, but maybe he is."

"Wouldn't be surprised if they put trackers on our vehicles."

"We'll get 'em sweeped soon as we can."

It only takes a few minutes to reach the warehouse where Pawie is waiting for us.

He's standing in front of a black Hummer in the empty parking lot of the abandoned warehouse.

Standing on either side of the vehicle are two mercenaries in black fatigues and gear, including sidearms and aviator shades.

As we pull up, he walks out to meet us, putting about twenty feet between him and his men.

He's a small man in a suit, which makes him look like a child. Like his rent-a-soldiers, he sports a military-style haircut and aviators.

"Thanks for meeting me," he says, extending his hand.

His handshake is overly firm, but his hand is so small it's barely noticeable.

"I want you to know that I respect what you do. We're in a

similar type profession—security, investigation, and enforcement outside of government agencies. We do what they can't. And from what I hear and read y'all are good at what you do just like me. I feel terrible about what happened and I want to help. The thing is . . . it was only recently brought to my attention. I've been overseas overseeing various operations and was only told about the situation when I returned. Unfortunately the only ones even aware she was missing were local support staff and they didn't handle it properly. But now that I know . . . Well, she was only a glorified receptionist, but she was one of our employees. We can't have our employees goin' missing. It's not good for business. If you had any idea of the operations we're running or assisting in around the world and the stakes involved . . . The thing is . . . rather than conduct our own investigation and duplicate the things you've already done or try to do what you're better at doing anyway . . . we'd like to offer our support and considerable resources to you and your investigation."

He reaches into his pocket, pulls out a small jump drive, and hands it to me.

"Here is all the information we have on her—her employee file, her background info, work records, and video footage from the final time she ever came to our offices. I'm trusting you with some sensitive information because everything I'm being told is that I can, that you are discreet and know what you're doing. Anything you need at all just let me know. We can help with surveillance, security, information, you name it. We just have to be kept out of it. We need you to keep our name out of every aspect of the investigation. It's a matter of national security and it's no exaggeration to say that global stability is contingent on you doing so."

I nod as if I agree and am going to comply. "What can you tell us about her?"

"Only what I've been told. I never met her. Her supervisor says she was a good worker. Reliable. Loyal. The only thing of note is how many questions she asked. Evidently she really grilled many of the field guys about techniques and strategies but since it seemed to be for her own personal safety and security it didn't raise any red flags. Maybe she knew she had a stalker or was tryin' to get out of a bad relationship and was preparing for the worst. Maybe that's what happened to her. Probably is. Definitely most likely. I just wish she would've let us know so we could have dealt with it and kept her safe. I understand her fiance is a detestable deviant. Is he?"

"A detestable deviant? I ask. "Is there any other kind?"

"Right. Well, we're set up on him. If he has her we'll know soon enough. Or if he does anything we'll know and we'll let you know. In the meantime . . . read her file and watch the video footage and get back with me with any questions you have or any other way in which we can help. I leave for Ukraine in a few days. Let's try to get this wrapped up by then."

CHAPTER
FORTY

"HOW MUCH OF that bullshit did you believe?" Blade asks.

"Not much."

We are back in the car driving into town.

"Why didn't you ask more questions, pump him for more information?"

"I wanted to learn what he had to say and hear what narrative he was pushing."

"Fuckin' global stability," she says. "Think anything he said was true?"

I shrug. "I'll be interested to see how he answers our questions and what following Owens produces."

"Little man syndrome much?" she says. "He's like a kid playing army with real toy soldiers."

"You know . . ." I say. "*He's* small enough to be the man on the video."

Pete calls and I answer it.

"Y'all done? Thought you were going to call me back."

"Sorry. Just wrapped up a few minutes ago."

"*And?*"

I tell him.

"Nice to have his help," he says.

"But is it?" I say. "Is it actual help or a way to try to control the investigation? He didn't ask us if we wanted Owens surveilled. He just did it. And I'll bet you Blade's left nut there's nothing on the drive we don't already have or know."

"Only I can bet my nuts," Blade says. "But I bet it's a pretty safe bet."

"When did y'all become so cynical?" he says. "What's your next move?"

"Headed back to talk to Rayden Payne again. Gonna see if he'll let us look around his house."

"Call me if he has her."

When we pull up to PCPC we see that the store is closed.

There's no sign on the door or explanation, but all the lights are off.

Blade pulls out her phone and checks its hours of operation. "Supposed to be open."

"Suspicious," I say. "Let's go see if he's home."

"If he's left town with her after we interviewed him . . ." Blade says.

"Maybe he's just under the weather today."

It's a short drive to Payne's house.

He lives in an old, small cinderblock home on a little lot in a neighborhood behind Target farther down on 23rd St.

The cinderblock has been painted a bright blue that matches the tarp covering the right side of the roof.

Though not uniform, many of the homes surrounding Payne's are similar.

Unlike most of them, his car is in the driveway. His is also the only house in the vicinity that doesn't have some kind of Christmas decoration.

Blade says, "Maybe his ass is really just sick."

"Let's go find out."

We park behind his car and get out.

After ringing the doorbell and banging on the door for a few minutes, we call his number. Like the doorbell, we can hear his phone ringing inside the small house, but there is no other sound.

Blade says, "Ray, we know you're in there. Open up. Don't make us fuck up your front door."

"I'm gonna walk around back," I say.

I walk around the right side of the house to the tiny backyard. Like the front yard, there is more dirt than grass, and the only item in the entire area is a leaning and rusting gas grill missing the propane bottle.

When I find that back door unlocked and slightly ajar I call Blade and let her know.

In less than twenty seconds she's standing beside me looking at it.

"We goin' in?" she asks, but I knew it wasn't really a question.

I dig a pair of latex gloves out of my pocket and put them on. She does the same.

Pushing the door open the rest of the way I call out for Payne, but I could've saved my breath.

The pungent wet-copper smell of blood wafts over us.

Blade pulls out her small, snub nose .38 from the holster around her left ankle.

"That your blood, Ray?" Blade says as we step inside.

The backdoor opens into a small dirty kitchen. Plates with remnants of breakfast still on them on the table, blue pots and pans in the sink.

"Maid's day off, Ray?" Blade yells.

"More than one plate on the table," I say.

"Either Ray entertained last night and it went well or . . ."

We slowly make our way through the kitchen and into the living room, which puts it on the other side of the front door we were just banging on a few moments earlier.

The living room is furnished with old, dusty furniture, the couch and recliner of which are draped in ill-fitting slip covers and littered with electronics, wires, tech magazines and books, manuals, and other clutter.

Making our way down the narrow, short hallway we come to the bathroom first. Barely big enough for the small yellow porcelain tub, the white porcelain commode, and the green porcelain pedestal sink, the tub and tap are dripping and everything is about as clean as an unattended outdoor gas station restroom, but no one is inside.

The final two doors are at the end of the hallway, one on either side, both closed.

As we get closer, we can see that the one on the right has a hasp and a padlock on it.

"Knew we shoulda come here and not just gone to his business," Blade says.

"Rookie mistake," I say.

The hasp is not fastened and the open pad lock dangles through the staple loop.

"If she was alive when we spoke to him at the shop and is not now . . ." Blade says.

"We don't know for sure he—"

"Yes, we do."

"Let's check the door to the left first," I say.

It is the one without the hasp and lock.

I push it open as Blade stands pointing her weapon into it.

It's obviously Payne's bedroom.

The small room has an unmade double bed, a single, flimsy dresser with an empty frame where a mirror once hung, and a shallow closet with no door.

The room is cluttered with clothes and computers and trash.

We check under the bed and in the closet and behind the dresser. No one is in the room.

Stepping back into the hall, Blade raises her weapon and I push the other door open.

The room is empty apart from a soiled blanket, chains bolted to the wall with hand cuffs and shackles attached to them, and the lifeless, bloody body of Rayden Payne crumpled against the right wall.

He's in a seated position, his back leaning against the wall at a slight rightward angle, his head drooping forward and to the left.

He appears to have been stabbed repeatedly with a large kitchen knife, which is still protruding from a spot between his left shoulder and chest.

"She got your ass good," Blade says to the corpse.

"Someone got him," I say.

"It was her," she says. "And I'm so glad she did. We failed her but she didn't fail herself."

"Let's back out of here and call Pete."

CHAPTER
FORTY-ONE

"HE ALWAYS KEPT TO HIMSELF," Carol Barry is saying. "Sort of quiet and shy. He'd wave from across the street or say hi if we both happened to be checkin' our mail at the same time. But that was it."

Carol Barry is an elderly white woman with glasses on a string that keep slipping to the end of her nose and a bird's nest of gray hair standing high on her head.

She has been Rayden Payne's neighbor for as long as he's lived across the street and the only neighbor we've been able to find at home so far.

She is standing on her stoop next to a small, plastic manger scene so faded that Jesus, Mary, and Joseph appear to be apparitions.

Across the street, Payne's place is surrounded by emergency service and law enforcement vehicles, all with their lights still flashing. Inside, FDLE is processing the crime scene.

The Florida Department of Law Enforcement is a state agency that assists smaller, local agencies with a variety of forensics and investigative support.

"What happened over there?" she asks. "Is he okay?"

"That's what we're trying to find out," I say. "The what

happened part. As to the is *he okay* part . . . Rayden is no longer with us."

"He's dead?"

"I'm afraid so."

"Wow. How?"

"I'm sure the sheriff's office will release a statement as soon as they can."

"Bet it wasn't natural causes," she says.

"What makes you say that?"

"He was so young," she says. "And . . . I don't know. Something about him wasn't right."

"Like what?"

"It's nothing specific. More just a feeling. It's hard to explain."

"He ever have any company?" I ask.

"Not often. A girl occasionally. To be honest . . . they . . . I think they may have been prostitutes."

I nod.

"Probably were," Blade says.

"Anybody recently?" I ask.

"You know . . . I thought he might have someone over there, but I haven't seen anyone."

"What made you think he might have someone over there?" I ask.

She shrugs her sloping shoulders. "Don't know exactly. Just something about the way he was acting, the schedule he was keeping. He stayed in a lot more. Didn't go out to all hours like he used to. And . . . I don't know."

"What?"

"It may be nothing, but . . . he'd leave his car parked in his driveway and walk somewhere. I'm not sure where, but he'd do it nearly every day. Just walk out of his house and down the street and disappear for a short while then come back. A few times he came back with a Target bag but most of the time he was empty-handed. I know it's not that strange or anything but it's very out of the ordinary for him. Never done anything like that before and now he's doing it every day."

"What about vehicles?" I ask.

"Any besides his over there in the past week or so?"

"You know . . . there was one a while back. It was in the middle of the night. It was there when I got up to go to the bathroom, but gone the next morning."

"Do you remember what kind of car it was?"

"No. It was dark. Couldn't make it out too well."

"Thank you. You've been very helpful."

"He wasn't robbed, was he?" she asks.

"We're not sure, but we don't think so. Why?"

"Am I at risk here?"

"We believe it was an isolated incident," I say. "Just use normal precautions. Keep your doors locked and your eyes open."

CHAPTER
FORTY-TWO

"HE HAD someone chained up in there—probably several someones over the time he's lived there," Pete says, "but . . . we have no idea who. There's probably DNA on the cuffs and blanket, but with no one to match it to . . . it won't do us any good. We'll collect prints and see if we get any matches, but they'd have to be in the system. So right now we don't have a lot. We don't even know if whoever was chained up is who killed him."

Pete, Blade, and I are standing on the closed off street in front of Payne's house outside of the cordon. It's later in the day and he's giving us an update before we head to the sheriff's office to give our statements.

"The hell we don't," Blade says. "I know it was her."

"The same way you knew Silas Segal was the guy?" Pete says.

"He's right," I say. "We think it was her, but we don't know for sure, can't know for sure yet."

"I'm tellin' y'all it was her."

"Then where is she?" I ask.

"She got free and got the hell up outa here. Took him out in the process."

"Where'd she go?" I ask. "How'd she get there?"

"Her car, probably."

"You think her car was here?" Pete says.

We both nod.

"Neighbor saw a vehicle around the time when we think he grabbed her," I say. "It was only there a little while in the middle of the night, then gone the next day."

"Then how did she—"

"He's been walking somewhere for a short while every day," I say. "Probably to crank and move her car."

"Blade says, "Probably had it in the Target parking lot. Moved it around each day. If she didn't take it, it's probably still there. But she probably put it together that there's where it was when she saw him coming back with Target bags occasionally. If her purse and keys were in the house all she'd have to do is walk over there and use her car alarm to find it."

"I've called the hospitals and put out a BOLO," Pete says. "Nothing so far. I'll update it to include her car."

"We need to contact her friends and coworkers and ask Brousard if she's reached out to Owens," I say. "Check with Powers too—in case they really are as close as he claims."

"Let's do that," Pete says. "No tellin' what kind of shape she's in. If it's her."

"It's her," Blade says. "I'm tellin' you."

CHAPTER
FORTY-THREE

"NOPE, YOU KNOW SHE'S NOT," Gerald Powers is saying. "You just searched the place."

We are at his home, paying him a surprise visit after giving our statement and being interviewed at the sheriff's office.

"So she's not here?"

"You know she's not. What is this? Did y'all forget you just searched the place a few hours ago?"

"Has she contacted you?"

"No."

"Would you tell us if she had?" I ask.

"Not if she didn't want me to. Why are you asking me all this?"

"There's a chance someone was holding her and she escaped."

"Really? Who? Is she okay?"

"It's just a possibility we're looking into. We don't know for sure. If she does get in touch, please let us know. Even if she doesn't want you to. It could save her life."

"Can't promise anything, but if she'll let me I will. And if she needs help I'll give it to her."

. . .

We can't find Keisha Barjon, but after several attempts she answers our call.

"What is it?" she says. "Now's really not a good time."

"Have you heard from Charlotte?"

"What? No. How would I—"

"We haven't confirmed this yet, so we don't know anything for sure, but we think it's possible that she was being held by someone and recently escaped."

"Really? Who?"

"We can't say yet. We don't have any confirmation on anything. This is just a theory we're exploring."

"The guy on the news?" she asked. "The one that . . . Did she kill him to escape?"

"If it was her she may reach out," I say. "Please let us know if she does. She's not safe and needs medical attention. Please call us the moment you hear from her. Even if she doesn't want you to. She'll be in shock and won't know what she needs. It's a matter of life and death. Please let us know."

We approach Crystal aka Brandy Haines in the parking lot of Cloud Nine where she has just arrived and is preparing to go in to work her shift.

"Have you found her?" she asks.

"Maybe," I say. "We're not sure."

"What does that mean? Oh, no," she says, covering her mouth, "is she . . . Do you have a Jane Doe and—"

"No. But we think it's possible she may have been being held by someone and recently escaped."

"Wasn't Len, was it?" she asks, referring to Len Jennings her abusive boyfriend who Charlotte was trying to get her to leave.

"We don't think so," I say.

"Good."

"Has she tried to contact you?"

"No. I wish she would. I've been worried sick."

"If she does get in touch please let us know as soon as possible. It's extremely important. She's in danger and she's in shock. She won't be thinkin' straight."

"Will do. God, I hope she's okay. She's been through so much."

"How you know what she been through?" Blade asks.

"No, I don't. I meant long before she disappeared. I'm talkin' about all the family tragedy—losing her dad and sister. Havin' an abusive husband and then . . . bein' with that . . . Owens creep. That's all I meant. I have no idea where she is now or where she has been. I just pray to God she's okay."

We meet Clyde Brousard at the St. Andrews Marina.

It's cold and windy, the breeze blowing in off the bay, snapping sails and flags, clanging rigging, and watering our eyes.

I tell him what we know and what we think.

"Has she reached out to Owens?" I ask.

He shakes his huge head. "Far as I know he hasn't heard anything from her and didn't have anything to do with her disappearance. Now, I ain't with him twenty-four-seven and don't know everything about what he gets up to, but I'm with him more than anyone and I ain't seen anything that makes me think he had anything to do with it. *And* . . . he really seems to be workin' hard to find her."

"Yeah," I say. "We could be wrong, but it looks like Rayden Payne had her—"

"'Til she knifed his ass," Blade adds. "Guess all that info she got from the KLS mercs paid off."

Brousard says, "She always seemed tougher and smarter than she appeared to be."

"Turns out she was," I say.

"She was runnin' circles 'round Owens and he never suspected. She . . . everything she did was . . . She always knew what she was doing. Was always in control. She'd pretend not to be, pretend to be upset or emotional, but she never was. He thought she was. Thought he was winning an argument or controlling her in some way. Not once. Not ever."

"If she reaches out, will you let us know?"

He nods. "Hope she does. Owens was serious about the deadline he gave you."

CHAPTER
FORTY-FOUR

THAT NIGHT ALANA and I are playing the cups game when Pete stops by.

Ashlynn is on another date with the same online guy and Blade is at the kitchen table on her laptop.

The cups game, which Alana invented, involves us building castles out of red Solo cups and her in Godzilla fashion standing up and kicking them over. It's an enormous amount of entertainment for a few bucks.

When Pete comes in, Blade closes her laptop and joins us in the living room—Pete on the couch, Blade in the chair, and Alana and I on the floor.

"Longer it goes without any sign of her," Pete says, "less likely it was her he had chained up in there."

I nod.

"We aware," Blade says. "And you got nothin'?"

"Nothin'," he says. "No sightings. No hospital or walk-in clinic visits. No cell phone activity. Nothing. And maybe he not only didn't have her in there. Maybe he didn't have anybody. Just because we found him dead in that room doesn't mean someone chained up in that room got free and killed him."

"True," I say.

Alana and I place the final cups on our most recent tower and she jumps up and kicks it over, squealing as she does.

"And y'all ain't found nothin' else in the house that points to who he had in there?" Blade asks.

"Only thing we got is prints and possible DNA," he says. "Prints will take a few days, but DNA will only help if we have someone to match it to. I mean, same is true of the prints, but they're easier to get from work records and things. And they're quicker."

"His creepy little ass didn't keep any souvenirs?" Blade says.

"Not that we've found so far."

"Have y'all searched his store and all the computers there?" I ask.

"Store yes. Computers are going to take a while, but we have them. Well, FDLE does."

"What about another property somewhere?" I ask. "Or a storage unit? Something like that?"

"We're dissecting his life," Pete says. "If it's there we'll find it, but it won't be quick."

I have a thought that just sort of bursts into my brain.

"Something Brandy Haines said gave me an idea . . ." I say.

"That we should do to her boyfriend what Charlotte did to Payne?" Blade says.

"What if . . . We've been thinking that whoever Payne had chained up in there got free and killed him."

"Charlotte, yes," she says.

"But what if someone else figured out where she was and took her and took out Payne?"

"Like who?"

"Could be anybody, but KLS would be top on my list," I say. "If it *was* them . . . it was smart to use a kitchen knife and make it look like she did it."

"That's not bad," she says. "But it could've been anyone."

"Need to look at all the original suspects again," Pete says. "And anyone in her orbit. But . . . if it wasn't her . . . If Payne never had her . . . all we're doin' is wasting valuable time."

I think again about how something about Charlotte reminds me of someone and I almost have it but it's gone.

CHAPTER
FORTY-FIVE

THAT NIGHT I fall asleep thinking about the case and all we know.

Memories and moments and bits of conversation swirl around inside my head.

I have to say . . . There was more to Destiny than there seemed. She was . . . more complicated, more . . . she seemed like different women at different times. And I'm not sure any one knew the real her.

Any idea where Destiny is?

She went on a trip last week, but—

Did you see her when she came back?

Yeah.

How'd she seem?

She's been different lately. Not sure why. Just like . . . I don't know . . . more quiet, to herself.

I'm a PI. I've been hired to find Destiny.

I could tell you were different.

Any idea where Destiny is?

She's been different lately. Not sure why. Just like . . . I don't know . . . more quiet, to herself.

Did she say anything about the trip?

Not really. Said it was nice. But that's about it.

Do you know why she went or what she did?

She's very . . . private."

She . . . It's like she's a lot of different people—or can be. I guess workin' here we all are a little, but she . . . She was next level. I never knew who the real her was. Guess I didn't meet her.

She say much about her boyfriend?

No. It was so strange. He was in here one time with her and said something about them getting married and that was the first time any of us had heard about it. She's fuckin' engaged and never even mentioned it. We just thought she was givin' him the boyfriend experience like everyone else and then out of nowhere she's going to marry him. It was bizarre.

Did she say why she was marrying him?

Only one reason you marry someone like him. The money.

At a certain point I wake and am up for a few moments.

When I fall back asleep I dream about parts of my childhood I don't really remember.

I'm a baby in a basket being left at a small-town fire station.

Then I'm a toddler in a cheap roadside motel room where my mom is meeting someone to sell me in a black market adoption.

The Five Saints are singing "In the Still of the Nite," which Fred Parris wrote in the basement of St. Bernadette's Church.

Blade and I are back in downtown Brunswick looking for Charlotte, but we're kids in too-big adult clothes.

The doo-wap song is still playing, but now it's distorted with an exaggerated echo, as if coming from within a deep well.

I stir again and then I'm back to dreaming about Charlotte and the case.

You know how some people are good actors?

Yeah?

You know how you know they're good actors? Because you see how they are when they're not acting. Right? But with Destiny . . . it's like she was always acting. Always playing a role. Always in character. I know her better than anyone here and I don't know her at all.

I believe I saw her, but can't be sure. See so many people each week.

Did she attend any of your activities or did you just see her on campus?

Just not sure. Sorry.

Do you happen to know what other groups were here last week?

Let's see . . . There was a singles group, some kind of corporate retreat, some Methodist youth groups from Ohio, a writers' conference, a grief recovery group, a women's conference, and a pre-marital counseling conference. I may be forgetting some. Last week was busy.

Can you tell us about her?

She's good people. A real sweetheart. Always enjoyed talking to her. Very smart. Always asking questions and tryin' to learn.

About?

Everything. She was fascinated by the work KLS does—the techniques, equipment, the dark work.

Dark work?

You know . . . the wet work . . . off the grid, outside the law, usually in other countries. Dark web, dark thirty. She may have just been flattering some of the operatives, but she seemed genuinely interested. I don't know.

Tossing and turning throughout the night, I have restless sleep and bizarre dreams and the next morning I have a new, unified theory of the case.

CHAPTER
FORTY-SIX

"I FINALLY FIGURED out who Charlotte reminds me of," I say.

"Oh yeah?" Blade says.

She is sitting at our kitchen table, a steaming cup of coffee in front of her.

"Yeah. Carrie Davis."

"The young girl Owens was druggin' who died recently?" she says. "Makes sense. He's got a type."

"I think it's more than that," I say. "I think they're related."

Her eyebrows shoot up and I can tell she's thinking about it.

"What if she did all she did in order to get close to Owens?" I say. "It's why she seemed like different people, why she would be more complex than she at first appeared. It'd be why she has so many aliases and her apartment is so blank and empty. It'd be why she was interested in techniques KLS employed. What if she was at St. Simon's for the grief group and what if the woman she was seen with in Brunswick was also a family member of the victim? Her mom maybe."

"So she's doing all this to get close enough to Owens to set him up or take him out and then—*boom*—Payne snatches her."

"It would also account for how she was able to escape, what she was able to do to Payne and why she hasn't resurfaced yet."

"Pretty good goddamn theory," she says. "Might just be right. How do we test it?"

"I asked Pete to track down Carrie's mother. We start with her."

"We could also follow Owens," she says. "But then what? Not stop her, right?"

"Hard to see her getting past Brousard," I say.

"So help her with him?"

"I'd rather not do that."

"You're not going to warn him, are you?"

"I don't know what to do," I say. "I could be wrong about all this. It's just a theory. I have no desire to protect Owens—just the opposite. But . . . I feel a certain loyalty to Brousard."

"I know he's helped us some and we probably owe him something, but . . . he works for Owens—by choice."

"I know," I say. "But think about some of the people we've worked for."

"Temporarily," she says. "And think about how many of them we've stopped working for when we found out more about them."

"Sometimes I think Brousard has stayed with Owens to keep him from hurting more people and to help us."

She shakes her head. "All we been through and you can have thoughts like that about people like him . . . I . . . You still surprise me sometimes."

"I could be wrong about Charlotte," I say. "She could be in a shallow grave somewhere, but if I'm right . . . warning Brousard might save Owens and get her killed and not warning him will break all trust we've built up and possibly get him killed."

"Easy choice for me," she says.

CHAPTER
FORTY-SEVEN

I MEET Brousard at our office later that morning.

"I need to say some things and ask you some things," I say. "Have a more direct conversation than we've ever had before."

He nods.

"I appreciate the position you're in," I say. "Especially between me and Owens. It hasn't been easy, but you have been helpful when you didn't have to be. I think you're a good guy working for a bad one."

"How else they gonna be stopped?"

I nod. "And I know you've stopped him from doing a lot more bad shit than he has. And I owe you more than I can ever repay for your help protecting Alana from Dimitri and company."

"But?" he asks. "Sounds like a but is coming."

"No but. I just wanted to thank you for all you've done."

He nods. "Well, let me do something else. I really think Owens is serious about the two days timeframe he gave you. Seems like he really is going to turn over the evidence he has on you."

"So that gives me one more day."

"I've looked for it," he says. "Thought I could help it get

misplaced or lost or some shit like that, but I haven't been able to find it."

"I really appreciate you lookin'."

"Do you have anything you can give him to keep him from . . . sending you back?"

"No. Not really."

A frown forms on his face and he nods his huge head slowly.

"Mind if I ask you a few direct questions?"

He shakes his head.

"Would you consider stopping working for Owens?"

"Consider it all the time."

I nod.

"But," he continues. "All I have is my reputation. If I quit a client word gets out . . . Nobody else'll hire me. The work I do . . . it's usually for . . . not the best people. I provide security, safety. That's all I do. I work for criminals sometimes, but I'm not involved in any criminal activities."

"What would you do if a victim of Owens came after him?"

"You mean you?" he asks.

"No, not me. But let's say he sends me back to prison or has me killed. If someone wanted to square it . . . would you . . . What would you do?"

"You mean Blade?"

"No. Not me or Blade but another victim and their family."

"My job is to protect my clients. That's what I have to do. But . . . if it was y'all . . ."

"Would you use lethal force?"

"With y'all?"

"No. Someone else."

"I'd try not to. Always try not to. Sometimes it can't be helped."

My phone vibrates on the desk. It's Pete.

"I need to take this," I say.

"Want me to step out?"

I shake my head. "No need."

I answer the call.

"Found the mom," Pete says. "She's in town and wants to talk to you."

"In town?"

"She's here lookin' for her daughter."

"Charlotte?"

"She's on her way to see y'all now."

As soon as I end the call with Pete I call Blade.

"Where are you?"

"On my way to the office."

"Carrie's mom is on her way to see us."

"From Brunswick?"

"She's already in town."

"Be there in a few."

When I end the call, Brousard looks at me, his face a big question.

I give him a brief summary of what I think is going on and how Carrie's mother also being Charlotte's mother might just confirm it.

"So all that before was you wonderin' what I'd do if Destiny comes after Owens?"

"Yeah."

"Makes more sense now."

"And?"

"Are you the detectives lookin' for my daughter?"

We turn to see a middle-aged woman who looks like an older version of Charlotte standing in the doorway.

CHAPTER
FORTY-EIGHT

"YOU CAN'T IMAGINE what that monster did to our poor Carrie and our family," Davis is saying.

She is seated next to Brousard in our client chairs. Blade is seated at the desk and I'm sitting on the edge of it, one leg on the desk, the other on the floor.

Brousard had offered to leave when Sarah came in, but I asked him to stay.

Blade says, "We're the ones who found her and stopped him."

"Really?"

"Burke here beat him to within an inch of his life and went to prison over it."

"Thank y'all for what y'all did, but . . . it was . . . just an inch too short."

"Did Charlotte move here to . . ."

"Do what the cops wouldn't do? What her dad would do if he was still here? Yes. She shouldn't have had to. And I didn't want her to, but . . . he murdered our little girl. He drugged her and abused her and did so much damage she could never get over it. We tried everything. But all we could do was watch help-lessly as she died a slow, painful death. He had already killed her. Just did it in way that let us watch in slow motion as she died. I understood why Char felt like she had to do what she had to do." She looks at me. "You get it, right?"

"More than you know," I say.

Blade says, "We all do."

"Have you spoken to her since she was at St. Simons?" I ask.

She shakes her head. "That's why I'm here. Trying to find her. Can y'all help me?"

"We think we're getting close," I say. "Is there anything you can tell us about where she might go or who she might stay with?"

My phone vibrates in my pocket and I pull it out. It's Pete.

"Sorry, I need to take this. May be news about Charlotte."

"Sure. Of course."

Pete says, "Just found Len Jennings dead."

I pull the phone away from my face and tell Brousard and Blade, "They just found Len Jennings dead."

"Who?" Sarah asks.

"The abusive boyfriend of a young woman Charlotte has been tryin' to help," I say.

When I put the phone back to my ear, Pete says, "She's settling scores. Got nothing to lose. Even money she goes after Logan Owens next. FYI. We have to warn him."

"Thanks for letting us know, Pete. Really appreciate it."

When I end the call, I say, "Pete says they have to let Owens know she's—"

Brousard pulls out his phone and looks at it.

"It's too late," Sarah says.

"Were you here to keep us away from Owens?" I ask.

"Of course not," she says in an insincere voice. "I'm just looking for my missing daughter."

"Wastin' your time to try to keep us away," Blade says. "We wouldn't try to stop her."

"Might just be too late," Brousard says, looking at his phone. "I missed a 9-1-1 text from him."

"A what?" Blade asks.

"When he has a situation he needs me right away for he texts 9-1-1."

He stands and heads for the door.

"We comin' too," Blade says.

The three of us rush out, leaving Sarah Davis sitting alone and calling after us, "You're too late. The monster is dead by now."

As we reach the parking lot, Brousard says, "I've got to protect my client. I don't want to hurt her or y'all, but I can't just let her kill him. Or y'all."

Blade glances at me with an *I told you so* expression. "Seems someone was just saying that this morning. Who was that? Some smart and good looking bitch."

"Please just don't get in my way," Brousard says.

"Shit," Blade says, "sounds like we all better be concerned 'bout gettin in her way."

CHAPTER
FORTY-NINE

LOGAN OWENS LIVES by himself in a huge, old restored and renovated home on Beach Drive with a glass front Florida room and a magnificent view of the bay.

Brousard arrives first. Blade and I close behind him.

When we enter, we find Owens seated in a plush recliner and Charlotte behind him with a gun to his head.

Owens is beaten and bloodied, his face swollen. His thin, pale body appears to have been stabbed repeatedly and beaten with a blunt instrument. His freaky light blue eyes are wet and tracks of tears snake through the drying blood on his face. His bleached-blond hair is crimson and his clothes and the chair he's in are smeared with streaks of wet blood and clots of coagulating blood.

Charlotte's tall frame is half crouched behind the recliner for cover. Her once platinum blonde is dirty and blood streaked, its extensions mostly missing. Her face is full of old bruises gone green and plum and her signature airbrush spray tan and seemingly professionally applied makeup are missing.

She's using the chair for cover because Brousard has his .45 drawn and pointed at her.

"I'm sorry for your sister and all you been through,"

Brousard is saying, "but I can't just stand here and let you shoot him."

"Fuckin' blow her brains out," Owens yells.

His words are slightly slurred and I can't tell if he has been drugged or if its from the beating he's taken.

"Charlotte," I say. "We've been looking for you. Sorry we didn't find you sooner. It's our fault. We made the mistake of interviewing Payne at his store instead of his home."

She shrugs. "Doesn't matter. He won't be hurting anyone ever again."

"Just like Len Jennings," I say.

She looks at me, her eyebrows rising and a small smile dancing at the corners of her split lips. "He's . . ."

"No longer with us," I say. "You didn't do that?"

"I told Brandy if he tried beating her again she could do it and blame me for it. Good for her. Only leaves this sick little dick fucker right here."

She presses the barrel into his head even harder.

"I've never beat a bitch," he says. "Never even once hit or slapped one."

"What you do is far worse," she says. "Drug and dismantle their souls. Ravage and rape and brutalize them while they're unconscious and commit acts of psychological warfare on them when they're conscious."

"Missy," Brousard says, "put down the gun and I'll let you walk out of here."

"The fuck you will," Owens says. "I'm going to disassemble her piece by piece and scatter the parts in por-ta-pot-ties all over Bay County."

"Nothing like that gonna happen to you," Brousard says. "I'm gonna let you go, but I can't let you kill him."

"The fuck you mean nothin' like that's gonna happen to her?" Owens says. "I say what's gonna happen not you. You're not gonna let her go, you uppity . . . fat fuckin' . . ."

Blade says, "Uppity what? Ain't got the balls to say it, do you?"

"Charlotte," I say. "Listen to me. We can take care of this for you. You don't have to kill him. I know you want retribution and I get it, but . . . it's harder than you think to come back from killing someone."

"I killed Rayden and I'm feelin' just fine."

"You're still in shock," I say. "And that was self-defense, to escape imprisonment. Killing in cold blood is something different entirely."

"I have to be the one to do it," she says. "My life has been over for a while now."

"Just put the gun down and walk out of here," Brousard says. "Ask them . . . I'm a man of my word."

"I tell you what your words are," Owens says. "You're making the biggest mistake of your stupid gorilla ass life. You won't just not work for me ever again. You won't work for anyone in this town ever again."

"You just fire his gorilla ass?" Blade asks.

"I sure as shit did."

Brousard holsters his weapon.

"You're even dumber than I thought," Blade says.

"The fuck're you doin'?" Owens asks Brousard.

"Not my job to protect you anymore," he says.

"Charlotte," I say, "you can still walk away from this. We'll take care of everything, make sure he can never hurt anyone ever again."

She seems to consider it.

Owens says to Brousard. "You can have your job back. I'll keep you on. I was just . . . It's okay. I don't fire you. Now pull out your gun and do your damn job."

"Got no job at the moment," he says.

"Yes, you do. Quit fuckin' around and—"

As Charlotte considers my plea she lowers her weapon some.

Reaching into the recliner, Owens come out with a small handgun, a .9mm from the looks of it.

Leaning back he points it behind him at Charlotte before she can react.

I just got her killed.

Like so many times in my life and work I intervened in an attempt to make a situation better and only made it worse.

The loud *bang* of gunfire explodes in my ears and they begin to ring.

Owens drops the gun as his head explodes.

I turn to see that both Blade and Brousard had fired a round into his head before he could get a shot off.

Charlotte screams and drops to the ground sobbing.

Brousard steps over to her and helps her up. "Come on, missy, let's get you out of here. It's over now. You're okay. You're safe. You're gonna be okay."

CHAPTER
FIFTY

A FEW DAYS LATER, Alana and I are playing in the park when Blade walks up.

We are surrounded by colorful, old-fashioned Christmas decorations that at night are lit up and even more magical.

We haven't seen Charlotte or Brousard since they walked out of Owens' house a few days ago. And I'm not sure if we ever will again. But it gives me great comfort to know she's in such good hands—and that Clyde has someone to care for and protect.

We spent the first two days giving statements and interviews to the police.

It helped that the security system in Owens' home mostly corroborated our version of events.

The investigation is ongoing, but Pete is hearing that Blade and Brousard's shooting will be ruled self-defense. They do want statements from Charlotte and Brousard, but after seeing Owens' repeated rapes and assaults on his home movie collection and hearing what he had done to Carrie they have expressed no desire to pursue assault and battery charges against Charlotte.

Yesterday we accepted a retainer from Gerald Powers to

investigate the disappearance of Indigo Fontenot and we plan to start in another day or two.

As we've been playing, Alana has been revising her wishlist and letting me know what she wants from me and what she wants from Santa for Christmas.

"What do you want for Christmas, Aunt Blade?" she asks.

"I don't know . . . Maybe world peace or some shit like that. What do you want from me?"

"A real Sonic the Hedgehog."

"Where the hell I get somethin' like that?"

"Ah, duh, *you're* the detective," she says.

Her words and gestures have such attitude and the statement is delivered so perfectly that we laugh for several minutes, during which she repeats the phrase several times.

Blade's phone rings.

"Is that Santa calling?" Alana asks.

"Almost," Blade says. "It's Uncle Pete."

As soon as she says it I know he's calling about Lexi and it isn't good.

He always calls me. Rarely ever her.

"Yeah," she says. "We're in the park with Alana."

I pull Alana over to me and give her a big hug and hold her for a long moment.

She must sense my need to do so because she doesn't attempt to squirm out of it.

When she ends the call, I look up at her and our eyes lock, mine stinging from tears.

"Lexi," I say.

She nods. "I'm so sorry. Anything I can do? What do you need?"

"Right now," I say, squeezing Alana a little tighter, "just this. Just this."

ABOUT THE AUTHOR

New York Times bestselling and award-winning novelist Michael Lister is a native Floridian best known for his acclaimed John Jordan "Blood" mystery thriller series.

Michael grew up in north Florida near the Gulf of Mexico and the Apalachicola River in a small town world famous for tupelo honey.

Captivated by story since childhood, Michael has a love for language and narrative inspired by the Southern storytelling tradition.

Before becoming a full-time novelist in 2000, Michael taught high school, worked as a college professor and inspirational speaker, owned and operated a bookstore, wrote a popular syndicated column, served as a newspaper editor, operated a community theater, wrote plays and screenplays, and worked for a production company. He has lectured extensively in the areas of creative writing, film, literature, spirituality, and self-help.

In the 90s, Michael was the youngest chaplain within the Florida Department of Corrections. For nearly a decade, he served as a contract, staff, then senior chaplain at three different facilities in the Panhandle of Florida—a singular experience that led to his first novel, 1997's critically acclaimed, **POWER IN THE BLOOD**.

Michael is also the author of the Burke and Blade Panama City Beach PI series (**THE NIGHT OF, etc.),** the 1940s Jimmy Riley noir series (**THE BIG GOODBYE, etc.),** and the thrillers

DOUBLE EXPOSURE, BURNT OFFERINGS, and **SEPARA-TION ANXIETY.**

Michael is the recipient of two Florida Book Awards—for **DOUBLE EXPOSURE** and **BLOOD SACRIFICE,** respectively. His work has spent time on both the *New York Times* and the *USA Today* Bestseller lists, been translated into German, and adapted into stage plays. Currently, **DOUBLE EXPOSURE** is in development for a feature film and the John Jordan books for a TV series.

Michael lives in his beloved North Florida, where in between writing stints, he enjoys time with his family and friends, playing basketball, and making music.

JOIN MY VIP READERS' GROUP

Join my VIP Readers' Group Today by going to http://www.michaellister.com/contact and receive free books, news and updates, and great mystery and crime recommendations.

ALSO BY MICHAEL LISTER

Books by Michael Lister

(John Jordan Novels)

Power in the Blood

Blood of the Lamb

Flesh and Blood

(Special Introduction by Margaret Coel)

The Body and the Blood

Double Exposure

Blood Sacrifice

Rivers to Blood

Burnt Offerings

Innocent Blood

(Special Introduction by Michael Connelly)

Separation Anxiety

Blood Money

Blood Moon

Thunder Beach

Blood Cries

A Certain Retribution

Blood Oath

Blood Work

Cold Blood

Blood Betrayal

Blood Shot

Blood Ties

Blood Stone

Blood Trail

Bloodshed

Blue Blood

And the Sea Became Blood

The Blood-Dimmed Tide

Blood and Sand

A John Jordan Christmas

Blood Lure

Blood Pathogen

Beneath a Blood-Red Sky

Out for Blood

What Child is This?

(Jimmy Riley Novels)

The Big Goodbye

The Big Beyond

The Big Hello

The Big Bout

The Big Blast

(Merrick McKnight / Reggie Summers Novels)

Thunder Beach

A Certain Retribution

Blood Oath

Blood Shot

(Remington James Novels)

Double Exposure

(includes intro by Michael Connelly)

Separation Anxiety

Blood Shot

(Sam Michaels / Daniel Davis Novels)

Burnt Offerings

Blood Oath

Cold Blood

Blood Shot

(Love Stories)

Carrie's Gift

(Short Story Collections)

North Florida Noir

Florida Heat Wave

Delta Blues

Another Quiet Night in Desperation

(The Meaning Series)

Meaning Every Moment

The Meaning of Life in Movies

MORE: Do More of What Matters Most and Discover the Life of Your Dreams